"So it's a deal, then? We sleep together—in all senses of the word."

She supposed she should say no. Most other women would. Ha—that was a lie. Most women would leap at the chance to lie with Daniel night after night. His lover credentials were unbeatable. Physique plus technique equals *magnifique.* She just had to remember there was nothing else on offer here. Merely a deal to sleep with someone—two insomniacs having regular sex in the quest for a decent night's rest after. Anyway, she shouldn't want anything else—should she? Not from a shining example of the modern conservative establishment like Daniel.

"OK." She nodded. "Someone to sleep with." That was all he would be. Her bedmate.

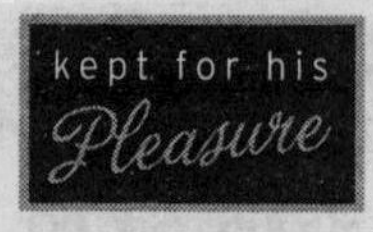

She's his mistress on demand!

Whether seduction takes place in his king-size bed, a five-star hotel, his office or beachside penthouse, these fabulously wealthy, charismatic and sexy men know how to keep a woman coming back for more! Commitment might not be high on his agenda—or even on it at all!

She's his mistress on demand—but when he wants her body *and* soul he will be demanding a whole lot more! Dare we say it...even marriage!

Don't miss any books in this exciting new miniseries from Harlequin Presents!

Natalie Anderson

MISTRESS UNDER CONTRACT

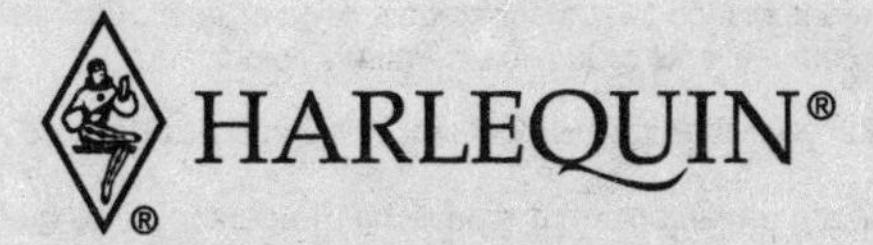

TORONTO • NEW YORK • LONDON
AMSTERDAM • PARIS • SYDNEY • HAMBURG
STOCKHOLM • ATHENS • TOKYO • MILAN • MADRID
PRAGUE • WARSAW • BUDAPEST • AUCKLAND

ISBN-13: 978-0-373-12810-5
ISBN-10: 0-373-12810-X

MISTRESS UNDER CONTRACT

First North American Publication 2009.

This edition published by arrangement with Harlequin Books S.A.

www.eHarlequin.com

Printed in U.S.A.

All about the author...
Natalie Anderson

Possibly the only librarian who got told off herself for talking too much, **NATALIE ANDERSON** decided writing books might be more fun than shelving them—and boy, is it that! Especially writing romance—it's the realization of a lifelong dream, kick-started by many an afternoon spent devouring Grandma's Harlequin® novels.

Natalie lives in New Zealand with her husband and four gorgeous-but-exhausting children.

Swing by her Web site anytime—she'd love to hear from you at www.natalie-anderson.com.

For Jo, the world's best Webmistress—thank you.

CHAPTER ONE

You always pre-plan your activities
You find putting things in order satisfying
You think that rational analysis is the best approach in all situations
You constantly monitor progress
It's essential for you to try things with your own hands
Objective feedback is always helpful
You enjoy an active and fast-paced environment
You have good control over your desires and temptations
You find it difficult to switch off from your job
You believe justice is more important than mercy
You enjoy the challenge of competition
You rely on reason rather than intuition
You make your decisions spontaneously
You like to have the last word
Intense emotions strongly influence you
You find it difficult to talk about your feelings

LUCY stared at the list of statements and wondered what it would tell about her if she answered 'yes' to all of them. Maybe she should alternate yes and no. Or maybe she should do some pretty mathematical pattern. Good grief. She was applying to be a hospitality temp. Why did she have to do a personality-type test?

As if there weren't enough forms to fill in? All the health and safety caveats, background checks, proof of qualifications… You'd think she was applying for a job with MI5. Not some tin-pot agency that supplied catering staff at short notice.

It was money *she* was short of. And this was her third agency of the day. She'd have been to more if there weren't so many forms to fill in. Now it was four-thirty and she'd be pushed to get all the paperwork done in time to complete an interview before closing.

She fidgeted with the clipboard and pen and the receptionist gave her a sharp glance. Lucy offered her a conspiratorial smile but froze it as she hit the woman's frigid response. 'I know the forms take a while to complete. I'll be doing some filing out back. Ring the bell when you're done and one of the consultants will come to interview you.' No smile, instead a look of condescension fluttered across the dragon's features as she walked out of the room.

Lucy nodded and quelled the urge to poke her tongue out after her. She looked back at the list and decided to try to get herself identified as a Type A personality—those aggressively ambitious, achieving, arrogant and frankly anal people who ran their lives according to deadline and tangible barometers of success. Lucy lived in a category of her own: Type F, for fun, flippancy, frivolity and freedom—not to mention occasional foolishness. She hummed softly as she started ticking various yes and no boxes, her smile returning full force as she worked through. It was so much fun pretending.

She heard a soft cough and looked up to see Mr Type A incarnate standing in front of her. She hadn't heard the door. Tall, dark suit, white shirt. Neatly trimmed brown hair. Cold eyes, staring at her, frown firmly fixed on the crisp-cut angles of his face.

Shame. Looks like that shouldn't be marred by bad temper. Her hackles rose. And it wasn't just because of the golden eyes sending her that dagger-like look. His aura stamped his impression on his surroundings and on her—height and breadth of a champion. This was a man who knew what he wanted and was used to getting it. He had the unmistakable air of 'Authority'.

The bane of Lucy's life.

Eyes narrowing, she stared right back at him. Defiant as ever in the face of someone so obviously establishment. But that didn't stop the kick of attraction roaring into life. She refused to allow anyone to have control over her, but for a split second she thought about what he'd be like in the driver's seat—just for an hour, just her body. He looked as if he'd know what to do.

She couldn't stop her little smirk.

His brows lifted and the look he was drilling into her underwent a subtle change. No less intense, still not friendly—but the sparks had a different quality. He looked again at the empty seat at Reception and back at her. What, he expected her to fill him in?

She bet he could do some filling. Good grief, was she really looking at a guy in a suit as if he were some hot dish? She swallowed and dragged her mind back to the situation. She'd never have picked him to be job-hunting. He didn't look like any bartender or waiter she knew and she knew a few.

She finally felt compelled to answer his unspoken question. 'The receptionist is filing out back but the forms are there on the desk. They take ages to fill in.'

His brows went another notch higher as he picked up an enrolment pack like the one Lucy was balancing on her knee.

'Start with the personality test. It's a cinch.'

He sat in the chair across from hers and flicked through the papers. The frown was back. His silence irked her. What happened to solidarity amongst temporary workers? Banter between bartenders was part of the deal. He skimmed over the list of yes/no statements that comprised the personality type form. And then he did speak. Sharp, quick, cutting.

'Let me guess. You'd be a "yes" for "you are inclined to rely more on improvisation than on careful planning". And a "no" for "it is in your nature to assume responsibility".' He waited for her response, his eyes issuing a hard challenge.

Her hackles were up again instantly. 'And I'm betting that you're a "yes" for "your desk is usually neat and orderly".'

His tight smile flared to a grin. She fancied she'd scored a hit, but then he sent the curveball. 'Maybe I should have made it clear that I'm not looking for work. I'm looking for a temp to work for me.'

'Oh.' Of course. What an idiot. Temps did not dress in made-to-measure suits and walk around with the assured confidence of a bona fide Greek god. But she rallied immediately. Spot the opportunity. Strike before they know what's hit them. 'What do you need?'

'Bar manager.' His eyes narrowed.

'Look no further.'

'You know the perfect candidate?'

'I am the perfect candidate.'

She saw his attention slide over her ancient jeans and skimpy singlet top and was fully aware that she was hardly looking perfect. And that he was thinking the same thing.

'You don't even know what the job is.' He mocked her.

'You just told me. Bar manager. I can manage a bar.'

A wolfish smile appeared. 'You can manage a strip club?'

Her jaw dropped. Now *that* she hadn't anticipated. He looked way too square for anything remotely grey—more your black and white kind of guy. Right, wrong, official, unofficial, permissible, forbidden. His world would be one of order—totally opposite to her freewheeling one of complete chaos.

He leant forward. 'No. Not a strip club. I'm looking for someone with experience. Someone who can handle *responsibility*.'

'I can handle responsibility.'

'You just said you were a "no" to responsibility.'

'No, you said that. I neither confirmed nor denied.'

Their eyes met. Squaring off like a couple of cowboys in a spaghetti western.

'Give me your CV.'

'Give me details of the job.'

OK, so he held all the cards, but she could bluff. Better than anyone.

The silence was steady as they waited each other out. She lifted her chin a little and saw him focus on her mouth as she did so.

She couldn't stop the tiny curve to her lips as his parted. He'd speak first. She'd known his politeness would win out—he was that type. Cool. In control. Icily well-mannered.

'Principesa. It's a small bar but popular. I don't want it to start failing.'

She'd heard of the club. A new one—opened on the scene during the year she'd been away. As he said, small, but definitely had potential.

'What's your interest? You own it?' Her incredulity was doing her no favours but she really couldn't see him in the centre of such a scene. Principesa was for night owls—party people. He had white-collar workaholic stamped all over him.

'My cousin owns it. Lara Graydon.'

She knew of Lara. Six foot something, looked like a Nordic goddess. Had been a diva in the Wellington social set for several years.

'She's gone to the States for a couple of weeks on a personal matter.' His grimace indicated his displeasure. 'Leaving me to oversee the manager.' The last two words were ground out through a rigid jaw.

'And the manager?'

'Was found rotten drunk slumped behind the bar this morning by council authorities who were called when the club failed to shut down at the required hour. Music was blaring and then I discovered discrepancies in the till.'

'And this—'

'Adds up to one sacked bar manager.'

Lucy had the feeling that far more minor transgressions would also bear the wrath of this man. He was not the kind of guy to settle for anything less than the best. 'So you need someone as soon as possible.'

He nodded. 'It's Wednesday today. I can get away with keeping the club shut for a night or two but it must be open again on Friday. I want someone in there right away to clean up the mess it's been left in. There isn't enough stock to last half a night. I want someone who can walk in and take over.'

'Why can't you do it?'

He rolled his eyes. 'Dressed like this?' So he could do irony. He elaborated. 'I have a day job—one that keeps me busy enough. That's why I need someone responsible to take over so I can forget about it until Lara gets back.'

'When's that?'

'Wouldn't we all like to know?' He shrugged. 'Shouldn't be more than a couple of weeks.'

There was a silence. She eyed him calmly while her brain worked furiously. She tried to ignore the fact that he was incredibly arresting and that his cool determination was intoxicating. He was bright, blunt and to the point and, frankly, he turned her on. Under that suit lurked a sense of humour. What else was hidden under that remote veneer? But a suit? Come on. She'd never been attracted to a straight A type before and now wasn't the time to experiment. She was flat broke and needed work—to start immediately. Manager would pay more, even if it was only a week or two. She could puff up the experience for her next job.

She quickly opened her dog-eared satchel and took out a copy of her CV, wishing the other fifteen copies weren't quite so obvious. She masked her unexpected nervousness by pulling her shoulders back and handing the paper over with an assertive flourish.

He took the CV, not looking at it until he'd held her gaze in a challenging stare for so long that she was finally forced to break it. Looking down and away, she instructed her lungs to inflate. For some reason they didn't seem to be working on auto any more. It was as if he knew exactly what he was going to find on the page. And he didn't think much of it. As if he knew she could do better.

Rebellion burned.

There was a long silence as he read it through. His face gave nothing away but she knew he was less than impressed. Well, who wouldn't be? Even she could admit it wasn't great reading.

Finally he spoke. 'Well, we have one thing in common.'

'What's that?'

'You're not big on commitment either.'

She blinked.

He looked back at the paper, obviously biting back a smile. He'd shocked her. He knew it. And he thought it was funny. She gritted her teeth to hold back her sarcastic response. She needed this opportunity and she wasn't going to lose it by mouthing off at him. She inhaled deeply before inquiring in a voice that screamed frigid politeness. 'What makes you say that?'

'You've not held a job longer than three months.'

'I've been at university until the end of last year. Student jobs, summer jobs. They never last long.'

'And this year?'

'I've been travelling about.'

'Why did you leave your last job?'

Why did she leave any of them? That boredom, that restlessness, that niggling feeling that she wasn't quite right for it. She tried, genuinely tried and was your average, dependable worker—with a short expiry date.

'You phone any of my old employers and ask for a reference. I've never taken a sick day, I'm happy to work double shifts. I guarantee they will all say nothing but good.'

'You've a strong sense of your own worth, then?'

Well, there was the biggest bluff in history. She was good but not great. More mediocre than marvellous. She'd never really shone, but she'd never really tried to. What was the point? She'd been pigeon-holed years before as someone who wasn't ever going to excel. The only prize she'd ever deserved was for biggest idiot. A blip in her personal history that had given rise to feelings of humiliation, inadequacy and fear—feelings that haunted her still, that coloured each world she tried to build for herself. Which was why she kept starting over. Ultimately she feared to try her best because she suspected it still wouldn't be good enough.

She leant forward, abandoning dignity in her desperation for dollars. 'Look, I can do this. I've been working in bars and restaurants for years. I know the suppliers. I know what works and what doesn't. Give me the job and I promise you won't regret it.'

She glanced at the clock. It wasn't far off five. She hoped like crazy the receptionist wouldn't walk back in. Hoped her luck would hold to grant her this one chance. 'I know the drill from the cleaning to stock management to handling stroppy customers. Been there, done that. And I can deal with staff.' She looked at him firmly. 'Bar staff work hard. I know exactly how hard and I know how to give them the respect and motivation they need to keep working that way.'

She didn't know if her argument was working, but she did know he hadn't taken his eyes off her. She'd seen him glance over her a couple of times but for the most part his gaze held hers. She found it incredibly difficult not to be distracted by his intensity. And by the colour of his eyes. She debated whether they were truly pure gold or brown with gold flecks. Either way they were unusual. And mesmerising. She blinked. Not going to go there. Not going to be distracted.

'If you want someone to run your club. Then you want me.'

CHAPTER TWO

You always pre-plan your activities

DANIEL GRAYDON sat back and let the words hang on the air. *You want me.* Awful to admit it but he kind of did. Which was surprising because it only took a second to know she wasn't his type, sitting there humming, smiling to herself, she was on another planet from his. He took a few more seconds to look her over and reinforce the impression.

She looked like an untamed gypsy and he was more your refined-preppy-girl kind of guy. She had the kind of tan that signalled lengthy hours on the beach. The low neckline of her singlet top revealed not even the hint of a bikini mark—an all-over-body tan? He banished the immediate mental picture only to focus on her long legs—wrapped in worn denim. Sizable patches on the thigh and knee showed where only a few threads remained before they'd finally fray into holes. He'd love to know if the skin under them would be as golden and soft-looking as that on her arms, her neck… God, he needed to get a grip.

He forced his attention to her feet.

Cowboy boots looked back at him. Brown, pointy-toed, wedge-heeled with patterns worked on the leather. He felt the reluctant smile tug at his mouth. He wondered if there were spurs to match, or if she had a whip—other than her tongue, which he was quite sure was capable of giving a good lashing.

Her CV had 'wanderer' all over it—your typical instant-gratification girl. She'd stick around while the sun shone but any hint of a cloud and she'd be off. A shining example of the 'what's in it for me, me, me?' gender. Daniel was all too familiar with women—they upped and left uncaring of whatever disaster they left behind. No sense of loyalty, responsibility, reliability. Which was precisely why he upped and left them before they had a chance to. Ordinarily, he'd have enjoyed saying no to her. But in this instance he didn't require endurance, he required immediate and short-term. Her self-confessed flightiness shouldn't be a problem.

He looked back to her face. She was staring at him. He could feel her willing him to take her on. But it wasn't the bold challenge that got him. It was the glimpse of someone desperate for the chance, concealed under the confidence. As a lawyer he'd seen that look many times before. The hidden desire—wanting someone to listen and take a risk. Even though they knew there was really no chance and they were just waiting for the refusal. It was the look that had him taking on clients when his caseload was already too full to handle. Pro bono at that. The kind of cases that had the senior partners frowning at him.

She was talking again. 'You've got nothing to lose and everything to gain. It's nearly five now—if you want someone to start tonight I'm your only bet. I can do this. Let me prove it to you.'

He glanced at his watch. She was right; it was nearly five. No time to hit another agency. Certainly not if they were all as inept as the receptionist in this one was. So what choice did he have? He had to have someone in there tidying up the mess tonight.

Her green eyes burned into him. He saw passion there, with defiance and determination. The words were out before he realised he'd even thought them. 'I'll give you three weeks. We go to the club now.'

The look on her face was one he wouldn't forget in a hurry. The sultry, sarcastic covering lifted to reveal a truly genuine pleasure—her smile wide and terrific and impossible not to respond to. His heart lifted. And then the delight shown in her full lips affected him in another region altogether. Groin region.

Not good. 'Right now.'

He stood, expecting her to do the same. She was on her feet in a flash, papers tumbling from her bag as she did so. She stuffed the CVs in, creasing them. He watched, heart cooling, thinking that if she was usually that clumsy she might need them again sooner than she thought.

A woman walked in from the back office. 'Sorry, I was longer than I—' She broke off as she saw Daniel. 'I'm sorry. Can I help you?'

He raised his brows at her, giving her the supercilious-lawyer look he reserved for smart-mouthed petty crims, happy to teach her a lesson in customer service. 'I'm afraid you're too late.'

She looked nonplussed.

His new bar manager followed up by giving her an evil smirk. 'I'm sorry. I don't have time to complete all these forms. I have a job already.' She put the long strap of her bag over her shoulder. 'Shame. You missed a good commission.' Then she bent and lifted something else she had parked beside her seat. A violin case.

He stood back and watched as she passed him, a swaggering cowgirl looking in complete control. Completely confident. He glanced back registering the dismayed expression on the agency worker's face.

'You know you're making a big mistake. It's much better to go through an agency for temporary workers.' She practically tut-tutted.

'For whom?' Daniel flattened. 'Employer, employee or middleman who needs the introduction buck?'

He turned and joined his temp who was now waiting for him on the street. They headed in the direction of the club. It was only a five-minute walk through the funky end of town. Students, buskers and suits vied for space in the cafés they passed.

'So is it a violin or are you actually Mafioso?'

'You think I'm concealing a dangerous weapon?'

He had the feeling she was a dangerous weapon, full stop. 'You know, you're amazingly trusting.'

'Why?'

'You don't even know my name.' He had hers. Lucy Elizabeth Delaney. Twenty-four years old. Bachelor of Music, second class honours. Held current driver's licence together with own ancient car according to registration details. Exclusive private boarding-school and not much advertised in the way of extra-curricular activities. He had the feeling she might have been too busy having some kind of social life to be tied down to the debating team or the hockey team or the school choir.

She ran a sharp eye over his suit. 'You don't look the dangerous type.'

'Appearances can be deceiving.' A little piqued, he decided to hit where he knew it would hurt. 'You don't even know how much I'm going to pay you.'

This time her glance stabbed. 'I know the going rate.'

He realised then that he didn't. Wouldn't have a clue. He didn't know a lot about this business—other than the price of a decent glass of wine. If he wasn't careful this woman would have him over a barrel. She might not want to stick at any job for long, but that didn't mean she wasn't sharp.

'So what is your name?' She was staring down the street.

'Daniel Graydon.'

Outside the club he pulled the keys from his pocket, jangling them in his hand for a moment. Was he really going to hand these over to a woman he'd known precisely twenty-seven minutes? Heart sinking, he realised Lara had left him in one hell of a mess. He had far too great a sense of obligation and responsibility and she knew it. She knew he would never let her club sink. He was going to have to stick around to make sure this was going to be OK. He was going to have to keep a close eye on his new employee.

Damn.

She climbed the stairs ahead of him. He kept that close eye on the way her curves filled out the denim jeans, on the way her hips swayed as she smoothly mounted each step.

Double damn.

Had he, for the first time in his life, just made a decision using his body rather than his brain? His brain was telling him to let her go and get on with it, but his body was telling him to grab hold and see what magic she could do. His fingers twitched, wanting to reach out and stroke her.

She walked into the middle of the floor space, the heels of her boots clicking on the wooden floor. He went to the bar and flipped the lights. Wanting rid of the late-night, fun feel. Back to business. She paid him no attention. Instead she took in the fridge behind him, noting the lack of stock.

'When did you want this open again?'

'I was hoping for Friday.'

He saw her swallow as she looked around some more. 'We have a lot to do by then.'

He turned the screws a little. 'No. *You* have a lot to do. I have work of my own to be getting on with.'

She turned to him. 'Accountancy or law?'

He wondered which she viewed as the lesser evil. From the way she'd covered the question in sarcastic flavouring he guessed she regarded both as less than marvellous options. 'Law.'

'Hotshot, huh?'

Modesty stopped him from answering that one honestly. 'Hard-working.'

She nodded. More to herself than him. As if he'd confirmed her worst suspicions.

She focused on the room again. 'Where are the current staff?'

'I'm really not sure. There's a list in the office at the back of the bar. I rang them to let them know it was closing for a couple of days and that the new manager would be in touch.'

'I'll get onto that right away.' She picked up a stained coaster from the nearest table. 'It could do with a little freshening.'

'Freshen away. Just don't do anything drastic.'

She raised her brow at him and he didn't like the cunning in her smile.

He glanced at his watch. He needed to get back to the office before Sarah thought he'd run out for ever. But he didn't want to leave this woman alone in the club. Not yet. He needed to get to know her a little. He was used to reading people. It was part of his job. Not only did he have to understand the law and be able to apply it, but he had to understand people as well—understand the motivations, desires and reasons behind drastic action. But he'd yet to get a handle on her. She seemed a contradiction. Edgy on top, eager underneath. 'I have to get back to the office to grab some files.'

'Files?'

'I thought I'd catch up on work here while you start to get things sorted. Be here to answer any questions you may have.'

'I thought you didn't know anything about running a club.'

'I'm a good guesser.'

Lucy stood firm and stared down her new employer—again. He didn't trust her.

'Sure.' She smiled. 'Go get them. I'll chase up the bar staff.'

He hesitated.

She gave him a withering glance. 'Don't worry. I'm not going to hock off all the furnishings in the half-hour you'll be gone.'

The thing was, he seemed to think she actually might do just that. She couldn't for the life of her think why he'd just employed her. Not when it was so obvious he thought she was a flake. It must have been a spontaneous decision and one he was already regretting. She could see it a mile off. He didn't even want to leave her in the club on her own for five minutes for fear she'd what—run off with the remainder of the stock?

She felt annoyed. Really annoyed.

OK, so she'd never held a job for more than three months. That wasn't because she wasn't a good worker. It had always, always been her decision to leave. Usually because she was bored. Because there was somewhere else she thought she wanted to be. And, OK, she mouthed off a bit. Sometimes. Most of the time. Like always. That way she could keep people at bay. Keep their expectations low. Keep herself protected.

She eyeballed him. Damn his judgments. He could stand there in his immaculate suit with his immaculate face that she was not noticing; he could stand there and just watch her.

He didn't think she could do this. Well, screw him. And that, she conceded, was the problem. She wanted to. Lust like you wouldn't believe. She wanted to strip him, lay him bare and watch the frozen look go up in flames. Utter foolishness. Lucy had learned long ago to at least try to put the brakes on foolish notions.

He reached into his pocket and pulled out a card. 'Call me if there's any problem. I'll lock the door behind me on the way out.'

She reached out, the casualness of her gesture totally undermined by the intensity of their sparring stares. Again, she had to look away first. It was like staring into the eyes of a lion—and she couldn't help feeling he was capable of the kill. She watched him leave. Listened to his sure steps heading down. Waited for the sound of the door closing firmly behind him. Then she expelled the breath she'd been holding onto for what felt like hours.

This was huge. Huge. How on earth was she going to pull it off?

She needed help. She flipped out her mobile, wincing at the single bar left on the battery indicator. Knowing she'd already IOU-ed the pre-pay provider and had about thirty seconds' worth of time left. She pressed the number and hoped for the best.

Fortunately Emma picked up straight away. 'It's me. I need your help. Phone me back on this number, will you?' She rattled off the number, thankful her sister had scarily good mental recall.

A minute later the phone in the club rang.

'Lucy, is everything OK?'

'Yep. Actually things are great. I got a job.'

'Another one? Where are you now?'

'Wellington.'

'What happened to Nelson? I thought you liked it there.'

'Oh. All those hours of sunshine. I started to go crazy.'

Emma's laugh floated down the line. 'Stir crazy, huh, Luce. When are you going to stick at something longer than a few weeks?'

'When it rains men. This is a big job though—bar manager.'

'Really? Fab. What do you need me for?'

'I've got to get up to speed with the stock management systems and pay rolling and spreadsheets, Emma. *Spreadsheets.*' She hated the things.

Emma laughed. 'What systems are they using?'

Lucy looked at the computer and read out the programs on the desktop.

'Piece of cake, Luce, you'll crack them in no time,' Emma encouraged. 'Look, I've a spare laptop. I'll load the software on and send the guide with it by courier tomorrow.'

'You're a lifesaver.' Lucy gave her the club address. 'Controlling the ordering out front is no problem, it's the backroom stuff I need the handle on.'

'Good Lord, Luce. You know what?'

'What?'

'You sound motivated. Actually motivated.'

Lucy stared at Daniel Graydon's business card. 'I guess I am. I'm going to nail this job, Emma.' Because it was the last thing he expected. Three weeks was time enough to prove a point. She wouldn't just do the job, she'd shine. And once she had? Why, then she'd have a holiday.

'Good for you.'

She hung up, buoyed by the brief conversation. She walked back into the bar and stood in the middle—surveying her new domain. The club was up one flight of stairs, darkened windows overlooking the busy downtown street. A large pool table stood in one corner. Cosy nooks and comfy seating scattered around the edges, a small dance floor on one side of the bar with the DJ stand on the far wall. The space was small, intimate. It was made for selected entrants. It should be exclusive. Hip. She'd target the young, urban, wealthy—fashion designers, media lovies, movie technicians—and mingle them with the up-and-coming darlings of the political and judicial worlds. Wellington—New Zealand's city of power and privilege, flavoured with a touch of Hollywood.

And cool. Undeniably cool. Lucy understood the power of cool. Not that she was, but she could fake it as well as the rest of them. She could spot a trend. She'd suggested themes and altered décor a little in many of the bars and hotel restaurants she'd worked at over the years—and been successful.

Back in the little office she rooted amongst the chaotic paperwork for a list of staff details and started dialling. An hour later and she'd contacted all but one of them. A couple had already found other work, thinking the club was to be closed for a while, but the others were keen to get back to it. It meant she was short, though—and missing a doorman. But she could work long hours to cover the gap and she knew of the perfect bouncer. She might have been out of town for a year but she had some old friends she knew she could call on. She'd do all the calling necessary to make this work.

Her new employer provided premium incentive. For whatever reason—probably desperation—he'd offered her the chance. More to the point he'd laid down a challenge. Now it was up to her. And her appreciation of his stud factor was going to have to take a back seat to her proving him wrong.

CHAPTER THREE

You find putting things in order satisfying

'PULL together the files on the Simmons case, will you?' Daniel watched as Sarah, his junior, jerked up from contemplating her computer screen.

'I'm going to work off site for a few hours. Maybe a few days.' He could keep an eye on what was happening down at the club—just to be sure Lucy was going to be able to do the job she said she could.

'Off site?' Sarah echoed in disbelief. 'As in not in your office?'

He grimaced, her incredulity hitting a nerve. So he spent long hours in his office. Month after month he racked up the most billable hours in the firm. On top of that he did his pro bono work. Then he tutored and guest lectured at the university—they were nagging him to join the faculty full-time. He achieved—at a cost. The price was long days, every weekend. But he'd made the decision years ago to dedicate his energy to his career.

Sarah gathered the relevant documents while he ensured his laptop had the data necessary. He could always download more remotely if he had to.

'Are you needing me to come with you?' Sarah looked right into his face. He had the suspicion those brown eyes of hers were offering a little more than her legal services. He grimaced again.

No. Daniel never *needed* a woman. He might want one, in which case he'd have her, and then he'd move on, certainly never stopping to develop anything resembling a relationship. His parents had pointedly proved there was no such thing as for ever. No such thing as dependability or reliability. So Daniel had chosen career. He was focused and loving it.

He shook his head at Sarah. 'I can email you with any requests I may have.'

Early evening he climbed the stairs to the club, with an increasing sense of trepidation. She appeared at the top before he'd hit halfway. The hint of anxiety tightening her face faded as she saw it was him.

He raised his brows. 'Everything OK?'

She nodded. 'Staff are all organised and I'm just starting the clean-up.'

'You want a hand with that?'

She looked amazed.

He clarified. 'You could call in one of the bartenders to help you.'

'No. It's not that big a job and if I do it myself then I know it's done and I know exactly what's there and where it is.'

He heaved his bag onto the corner of the bar. It landed with a thud. 'A good manager delegates.'

'A good manager leads by example and is capable of doing everything herself that she asks her staff to do.'

She was in position behind the bar and he had to admit it looked as if she were made for it. Her hair hung almost to her waist. Long brown locks streaked with sun-kissed honey strands. Neither straight nor curly, it seemed in imminent danger of turning into DIY dreadlocks. It looked as if she'd been swimming for hours and then let it dry in the sun without bothering to brush it through. He had the crazy urge to reach out and grab it, wanting to see if it did smell of sea and salt and holiday. Behind the bar she was as relaxed as if she'd been parked on a beach all her life. Given her tan she probably had.

She picked up a cleaning cloth. He leaned over the bar and he saw the bucket of soapy water on the floor. Steam rose from it together with the smell of lemon-scented cleaning product. She looked at the bag he'd put on the bar, the files spilling from it.

'So you're a lawyer.'

He nodded.

'Commercial or criminal?'

'Criminal.'

'Prosecution or defence?'

He started to wonder if she'd had up-close experience with either. 'Defence.'

'So you're out to fight the cause for the wrongly accused. Justice for the underdog—'

'No.' He stopped her mid-flight. 'Actually, sometimes my clients are guilty. But they're still entitled to decent representation.'

'You're an idealist—the Atticus Finch of Wellington.' She caught his flash of surprise before he masked it. 'What, you think I can't read?'

'Why would I think that? You have a university degree. I know you can read. Whether you can think and apply is another matter.'

She gave him an evil stare. 'I'll have you know *To Kill a Mockingbird* was one of my favourite books in school.'

'So underneath all the mouth *you're* the idealist.'

She looked put out.

'What were your other favourite books?'

She shrugged. 'I don't remember.'

She turned to the glass shelves behind the bar and reached up on tiptoe to empty the top one of its bottles. Her body showed off to perfection as she stretched it out, only just getting her fingers round the base of the bottles. He couldn't stand to watch it.

'I'll get those for you.'

Her eyes flashed surprise but she said nothing.

It took him only a minute to get the bottles down for her.

Every cell in his body aware of how close she was as she worked to clear the next shelf down. He stood back and rested against the bar behind him, unashamedly appreciating her tanned figure. Broad shoulders framed a generous bust, tapering to a trim waist before flaring out again to round hips and a bottom that begged to be used as a cushion. Shapely thighs closely clad in faded denim—also perfect for cushioning a lover. She'd be soft, and hot and...he really shouldn't be thinking this way.

He couldn't stop.

He looked back down to her feet again. The cowboy boots amused him. Then he amused himself further by slowly looking back up her body with appreciation. While she wasn't plump, she certainly wasn't a stick figure—soft in all the right places. Smooth curves. Daniel liked curves.

The speed with which she spun round caught him by surprise. The move brought her closer and he found himself staring right at her breasts.

Oh. Yes.

He blinked and with a little reluctance brought his focus up to her face.

She looked defensive. 'You don't think I can do this, do you?'

'Why would I have given you the job if I thought that?'

'You tell me.' Her chin was tilted high in a challenge and all he could do was admire the long column of her neck—smooth, olive skin leading down to collar bones that begged to be kissed.

'You think I fancy you?' Damn. He did. He'd have to bluff. 'Sorry to disappoint you, darling, but you're not my type.' That was the truth. Really. She wasn't.

'Really?'

'I prefer a more...finished...look.'

'You mean plastic. Petite. Perfect. Arm candy for the hot-shot lawyer.'

He didn't even try to argue. She could think what she liked

so long as he was covered. And, yeah, maybe his dates usually were pretty perfect-looking things.

'Rankles, does it?' He leaned closer, resisting the urge to get close enough to touch her. Hell, he really wanted to grab and haul her to him. Regressing to prehistoric man minute by minute. Irritated, he went a step too far. 'By finished, I mean at least combed.'

The flash of hurt in her eyes had him instantly regretting it. Since when was he *mean?* He was like a kid in school picking on the girl he secretly fancied. God, he was never usually so gauche.

She blocked his glimpse to her soul by lowering her eyelids to half-mast, but her smart mouth and tilted chin were firmly up again. 'For the record. You're not my type either.'

'Really?' His muscles tightened.

'I prefer more…wild. Not square or…boring.'

'Bad-boy type who treats you mean, huh?'

'No need to be patronising. I'm not stupid, you know.'

No. She wasn't. She was smart—mouthed at least. He needed to back off. She was getting under his skin in a way he wasn't comfortable with. Having sex with her wouldn't be wise. Maybe when Lara was back and the responsibility for the club wasn't on him, he'd consider it. 'OK. So we're not each other's types. I'm glad we got that sorted out.'

She gave him one last look that swam in lack of interest and turned back to her shelves. He stayed exactly where he was and kept watching her.

Boring? She thought he was boring? What, because he wore a suit and practised law? She should learn not to judge a book by its cover.

She bent down and pulled up a trigger bottle. Sprayed frothy liquid on the glass and started to wipe it. She looked at him in the mirror behind the glass shelving. He didn't look away. Nor did she and after a moment her hand stopped ineffectually wiping the smears from one end of the mirror to the other. They stared.

What he'd love to do right now to show her he wasn't a square.

She must have grasped some hint of what he was thinking because suddenly she looked away and her wiping of the mirror resumed—a little frantically.

'I thought you had work to do.'

'Yeah.'

He pushed away from the bar and walked round to the other side, took the last seat at the bar and pulled out the relevant material from his bag. He put his laptop to the side and ignored it, opting for the paper files. Pen in hand, he bent to his reading. Determined to focus on the facts. Not be distracted by the beach-blown beauty doing the Cinderella act in the corner.

Lucy found cleaning the cooler cabinet a perfect way of working off the extra energy she seemed to have accrued. She watched him out of the corner of her eye. Half aggravated, half attracted.

So definitely not her type.

But so definitely gorgeous.

His head hadn't lifted from the pages he'd been intently studying for the last forty minutes. Good concentration. She could believe it. When he'd focused his attention on her she'd felt the full force of that intensity. He had the kind of look that went right through outer layers and into the heart of the matter. The heart of her. She wouldn't want to be on a witness stand and on the end of one of those penetrating golden-eyed stares. For a second there he'd had the look of a predator in his eye, out to conquer. Well, no one conquered Lucy, thanks very much. Especially not arrogant suits who made the rules without regard to the feelings and needs of others.

She couldn't stand the silence any more. 'Big case, huh?'

He lifted his head. 'Reasonably.'

'Are you going to get him off?'

'I'm going to do my best.'

He looked back to his pages. OK. It was like trying to get information out of the Kremlin. Mr Closed Shop. She had the urge to open him up. What would he be like out of the suit? What would he be like in bed?

Serious. Strong. Intense. Her whole body was on edge just from having him over five feet away. How fierce would her tension be if he were to get even closer—as close as a man and woman can physically get? And how complete would the relief be when that tension snapped?

Intuitively she knew it would be incredible.

She finished the area behind the bar and checked and double-checked the inventory of stock. She was tired from a long day walking round temp agencies and she was hungry but it looked as if Daniel was settled in for a long night over the books. How late did he expect her to work? She decided to give him a status report and wow him with her efficiency.

'I've organised the staff for Friday—they're coming in for a meeting tomorrow afternoon. Will you want to be here for that?'

He looked up, his eyes taking a moment to focus on her. When they did it was with deadly accuracy. 'I might be around—what time?'

'Three p.m. Meanwhile I'm looking into a replacement bouncer for the Thursday to Saturday shifts. I know someone perfect for the job.'

He didn't look impressed. He looked sceptical. 'Is he qualified?'

'Of course.' She couldn't wait to see his face when he saw her bouncer. Her imp of disobedience must have been obvious because he stared hard at her but refrained from comment. Lucy was disappointed; she'd wanted to tell him all about the black belt in ju-jitsu and six-foot-two physique. Instead he started the interrogation about everything else.

'What about the stock?'

'I've done an inventory and cleaned the shelves at the same time. I'll start contacting the reps first thing in the morning.'

'DJ?'

'Looking into it. Again, I thought I'd use my contacts.'

'What about the fire extinguishers and escape routes—got those sorted?'

She stared at him. 'Rules and regulations all you can think about?'

'We're not talking some small café here. We're talking a bar—late licence, heaving dance floor on the weekend. Health and safety is paramount.'

Well, for him it would be. He'd never see this place as a place to have fun. It was obvious it was all one huge headache to him. He was probably a refined wine-club kind of guy. All the law students she'd known when she was at university were going on about vintage and method and paying outrageous sums for a tiny glass of something sublime down at the exclusive bars on the fringes of the power enclave in central Wellington. 'OK, I'll check the fire exits.'

'I expect you to drill the staff in that. The last thing I'm having is some disaster on my watch.'

'Yes, boss.' There were risks to health and safety in any bar at any time. And she wasn't thinking fire or earthquake. There were other battles to wage and she'd ensure her staff were au fait with defence weaponry because that was one thing she did know about—firsthand.

He reached into his pocket. 'I got a key cut for you.' He handed her a slip of paper at the same time. 'This is the code for the alarm.'

'You're sure about this? You don't want to meet me outside?' She couldn't help the little bite.

His eyes flashed a warning but he spoke as if her tone hadn't registered. 'I have an important meeting tomorrow. I can't say how long it will go for. You'll just have to get on with it.'

She eyed him, very nearly clicking her heels and saluting.

He looked down at his spread files; she could see the way the contents were calling to him. The challenge of the earlier part of the evening had faded beneath his preoccupation. She reached behind the bar and retrieved her bag and violin case. Both felt heavy. She *was* tired and she wasn't looking forward to a restless night's sleep in the company of strangers.

He stood and stretched out his shoulders. 'You'll be OK getting home?'

She nearly laughed aloud. 'No problem.'

He nodded. 'Thanks.'

Maybe she had impressed him a little with the effort she'd put in tonight. Her sudden smile was warmer than she intended. 'See you tomorrow.'

He sat again, no sign of any softening in return. In fact, he frowned a little. 'You'll pull the door right behind you on the way out?'

'Sure.' Stupidly she was disappointed. She'd thought the least he could manage was a smile. Didn't smile much, Daniel. And why not see her out down the stairs? He couldn't even manage that small act of politeness. He really was as typical as she'd first thought. Arrogant and uncaring. His head was back down. She didn't think he even noticed that she was heading out the door.

Daniel felt as if he'd been reading the same line for about three hours. He listened as those teasing cowgirl boots started to trudge downstairs. He checked his watch. Just past ten-thirty . His frown deepened. He moved quickly.

'Lucy?'

She was halfway down already. She turned to look up at him, her hair hanging long down her back, her face shadowed by the overhead light.

'You're sure you're OK to get home?'

He saw the flash of her smile. 'Yeah. Thanks.' She paused. 'Thanks for the job, Daniel.'

'OK.'

He waited for her to descend, for the door to snib behind her.

Then he walked slowly back to his work. That smile was a knockout. He'd seen it—what, twice in the whole evening? Not the sarcastic, smart one that had edges sharp enough to cut glass. This smile had been huge and genuine and very attractive. He was in for a long, sleepless night and suddenly that smile was all he could see on the pages in front of him. Concentration obliterated.

CHAPTER FOUR

You think that rational analysis is the best approach in all situations

LUCY woke early after another restless night. She hated listening to the sound of others sleep. Always had. Even boyfriends. In fact she preferred her lovers to leave late in the night, giving her a few hours' uninterrupted attempted sleep time—alone, in silence and safety. Insomnia sucked.

Years of boarding-school had been a torment. Space and security were what she'd love. But the hostel in central Wellington was never going to offer either. A zillion backpackers made sure of that. She dragged herself out of bed, wishing sleep came easy. She'd had a fantastic dream at one point. Very fantastic. She'd been in the arms of one big, strong male and loving it. Then his features had firmed into those of her new employer. Daniel. Right at that moment three English girls had arrived loudly in the room. Good thing too. Explicit dreams about Mr Lawyer should not be happening. No way. He was so straight. So wrong. Not her type at all. But he made a suit more attractive than she'd ever have thought possible. And having him feature in her dreams was infinitely preferable to the shadowy figure who still haunted her periodically—turning her sleep time into terror time.

Fighting off the fuzzy features, the fuzzy memories that she'd never be able to fully recollect, she saw the queue for the bathroom in the hall and abandoned the idea of showering there. Pulling on her jeans and a tee, she grabbed her bikini together with her towel and toilet bag, stuffing them into her backpack. She wound her unruly mess of hair into a loose knot on the top of her head and quickly tripped down the stairs and out to the street below.

On the waterside of Wellington stood a fabulous swimming pool. An indoor haven for government workers and hip students wanting a complete workout. Lucy didn't really want to work out. She liked to walk along the waterfront but you'd never catch her running along it like the Lycra-clad bunnies and yummy mummies jogging with their baby buggies. Swimming, however, was different—a pleasure, a relaxant. Splashing in warm water, striking out with her arms and legs, the silky feeling of her hair as it fanned out. She loved the freedom of feeling her body floating—weightless, worriless. She could spend hours in a pool and often had. It was her second favourite thing next to dancing.

She scrabbled in her pocket for enough coins to gain entry to the pool, darted to the women's facilities, stepped out of her clothes and into her bikini. She didn't bother putting her bag in an automated locker—it wasn't as if she had anything of value to worry about losing. Her goggles hung loosely from her wrist and she padded barefoot to the poolside, dropping her bag on the bottom row of spectator seating. Swimming lanes were set up and general speed signs posted. On the far side a couple of men were striking out with great pace. Relentlessly they traversed the length of the pool, turning and heading back again, time after time, no pause for breath or thought. Like a duel they were chasing each other, one going up as the other came down the pool, and for a second she wondered who was chasing whom. They were a sight, with their strong arms powering through the water with ease, their faces obscured by the close-fitting goggles and the spray of the water. She shook her head a little to let her hair tumble free and then she quickly twisted it into a plait. Untied, the plait would work loose in the water after a few lengths, but that was part of the feeling of freedom she enjoyed.

The middle lanes were slightly more crowded—a greater number of average-speed swimmers. She chose the one with the fewest number of swimmers. Waiting for the last swimmer to be a decent distance she dived in, loving that split second between jump and splash where for that instant she pretended she was a dolphin diving in delight.

She swam a few lengths and after a time paused at the end for some deep breaths and time to float. The blood pumped through her body and she felt alive again—despite that lack of sleep. She stretched out her arms, laughing at herself. The number of times she'd gone to a day's work on little or no sleep must surely be in the hundreds, but it had never seemed to matter before. Today was different. Today she didn't just want to do her job, she wanted to do a *good* job.

She trod water at the deep end, checking the time on the clock, and replaited her hair. Then she struck out again for the far end, and with every stroke she tried to think about the club. For once in her life she was determined to do well. She wanted to prove she could—to Mr Type A himself. He'd given her the chance but perversely seemed doubtful she'd be able to pull it off. Well, she'd show him. And it was to Daniel that her thoughts turned time and time again. Instead of drink orders and duty rosters it was the man with the golden eyes. His height and physique thrilled her but those golden eyes threatened to be her undoing. If she wasn't careful they'd see right through her. Her aggression channelled into adrenalin and energy and she swam harder and faster than she had in ages. She tried to swim him out of her mind, forcing her focus back to the job again and again but failing each time. After a few more lengths, another couple of plaits, she was breathless and ready to get on with her day. She didn't want to be late. She reached up with her hands and with a push heaved herself up to sit on the edge of the pool, waiting for most of the water to slide from her body before she'd step over to her towel-covered bag.

She glanced along the pool and saw only one of the super-fast swimmers was still in the water, still stretching out with seemingly endless energy towards her end of the pool. She turned away towards her bag and stopped. There was a large expanse of bronzed, broad chest in her way. She blinked and looked up.

Golden eyes danced. Were they hazel or brown? Really she couldn't quite decide—either way the amber lights were incredible. She didn't think she'd ever seen such a colour before and they were most definitely wasted on a man.

Man.

Daniel.

Right in front of her and all but naked. Her jaw dropped. She knew it did and she tried to do something about it but the ability to make even that tiny movement seemed to have been stolen from her. Stolen by the five-hundred-per-cent male, male, male obscuring her path.

He was staring down at her. All of her. He wasn't smiling. Nor was he saying anything. And she felt the path of his gaze as if it had been his finger grazing her skin. Every slow inch he covered burned.

In, out. In, out.

That was how you breathed, wasn't it? Basic instructions to calm the shell-shocked brain. Except she was suddenly thinking about something else going in and out and what would it be like to have that body all about…?

Not good.

He looked up at her face and she tried to hide the saucy thoughts from his all-too-observant eyes. How long had they been standing there staring at each other like that? It had felt like eons but she hoped time had done one of those weird blips that it did every now and then—when what felt like hours had really only been seconds. Milli, mini, itty, bitty. Just like her bikini.

'Hi.' She might have smiled if he weren't looking so serious.

'What are you doing?'

Man, he was direct. Bordering on rude. And he made her feel as if she were doing something bad—just by his tone. She'd hate to be on the witness stand with him on the cross-examination team.

'Roasting peanuts. What do you think?' OK. Maybe it wasn't the best way to start the day with her new boss, but really.

Those gold flecks in his eyes sharpened. 'You like them dry roasted?'

'Yeah, with lots of salt.'

'I prefer mine honey coated.'

Well, bully for him. She grimaced. She bet he had a million wee honey-coated peanuts in his little black book.

'You swim for exercise?' His gaze quickly skimmed over her again.

'I swim because I like it.' Despite the fact he had the knack for getting her back up faster than anyone she'd ever known, he also had the ability to turn her on faster than anyone too—just like that. Just by standing there, too close. Too naked.

She felt mightily glad he had that towel draped round his waist. The mental images in her mind were dangerous enough. Speedos or shorts? Her brain presented a slide show of the various options. As the water trickled off him, she tried really hard not to watch the path of each droplet down the honed muscles. Whoever would have imagined the body he had going on under that shirt and tie? Incredibly broad shoulders, tight pecs and a light scattering of chest hair that traced down the defined six-pack abs and disappeared below the towel, an arrow leading to…well.

The silence had been a little long again so she jerked her attention back to his face instead of his body and broke it. 'You swim for fitness?'

He nodded. 'Always have. Used to compete. I swim here every morning and sometimes I swim in the outdoor pool near my work on my lunch break.' That explained the smooth golden tan that showed off those muscles. She didn't think he'd have the time for much sunbathing. She was impressed he actually took a lunch break. Then again, look what he did with it—worked out.

Competitive swimmer. Competitive lawyer. Over-achiever. No doubt about it, this guy was driven. And here she was wearing only the tiny bikini her sister had given her over summer. Her one item of designer clothing—a gorgeous hibiscus floral fabric cut in a way to flatter. Probably not standard indoor-pool attire if the serious one-pieces around were any indication.

'I've never competed. I just like being in the water.' She checked out the shoulders again. 'You were swimming in the fast lane, I guess?'

He nodded. Yeah. He would've been one of the two battling it out.

'You?'

'Oh, you know. Slow lane. Nice and easy.'

She was selling herself short. OK style. Outrageous swimsuit. Daniel had spotted that flower-covered bikini stretching out up and down the pool. She had a good technique. She had a great body.

Daniel had had many an exhausting session in the pool but he'd never felt breathless the way he did that very moment. He felt mightily glad he had that towel draped around his waist. Clinging wet swim shorts weren't much of a covering and with her standing so close like that his body threatened to show its appreciation of that bikini in the most basic way.

But he knew that already. The jeans and singlet top from yesterday had shown him that. But was it ever magnified today in the scraps of material clinging to her now. That bikini belonged on the beach. Preferably a private one with just him for company and a couple of refreshing drinks because, oh, boy, were they going to need them after…

He blinked. He wasn't having an erotic fantasy in the middle of a public pool, was he? He blinked again. Yes. Impossible not to when confronted with the vision of temptation before him right now. Her hair hung down her back in a loosely coiled thick wet rope. It gleamed darker when wet. As he'd suspected the day before, the tan was all-over-body. And the body was ripe—lush curves that threatened to spill out over the bikini bra cups. Soft rounded flesh peaked to hard nipples. He knew they were only budded from the cold of the water, but they were begging for a hot mouth to cover them, draw them in and tease them. His.

Frowning, he looked down, determined to shake this surge of inappropriate lust. No cowboy boots this time. Instead he saw perfectly painted toenails. Vixen red. Now that was appropriate.

He needed to get this conversation back on an even keel. 'I'm going in to the office but I'll see you at the club later.'

'Sure. I'll be there with bells on.'

That wasn't an image he needed right now. Not when he saw her decorated with tacky Christmas bell earrings on and nothing else.

He hesitated. 'You're OK to get back home?'

'Of course. You're going straight to work from here?' She looked surprised. Well, it was only coming up seven a.m. now.

He shook his head. 'No, I live on the parade. I always get a coffee at the café halfway along, then head home to change and get to work.' He didn't know where the suggestion came from; all he knew it was out of his mouth before he'd had the chance to think and keep it shut. 'Why don't you come with me and talk me through your plan of attack for the club?' He added a final bit to ensure he was coming on the boss, not just coming on. 'I'm assuming you've made some plans and have more ideas since last night?'

'Of course. I have a list to get on with today.' She wasn't looking at all comfortable. He realised she was still dripping wet and hadn't even had the chance to wrap her towel around her. Hell. He was stalling so he could check her out some more in that glorious bikini. Big mistake. Lust city was not his destination this week. He had a case to work and an obligation to fulfil for his cousin.

Mind you, she was hardly snapping up his offer. If anything she looked threatened. Why? She fidgeted—definitely uncomfortable. What was she hiding?

'Come on. Go get dressed. I'll get you a coffee. You look like you could use it.'

Her colour had drained, leaving her looking tired. More than a little intrigued, he gave her no chance to refuse. 'I'll meet you out the front in twenty minutes.'

She surprised him by being there in fifteen. He'd anticipated she'd be twenty minimum. But, no, she strode out of the change room only a second after he'd exited the men's. Her hair, still damp, hung in wild waves down her back. He'd said he preferred a more combed look. He'd lied. His fingers itched to rake through the mass, he ached to feel the strands trail across his face.

Her equilibrium appeared to be restored and the edgy look was back in her eyes. The look that said, Cross me and I'll have something to say about it. He liked to cross—he liked the sparring they'd had so far. Chin high, she raised her brows at him. Accepting her challenge, he turned and headed towards the door, expecting her to walk with him. She did. Satisfaction kicked. Adrenalin burned.

He stretched out at his usual pace—fast. He liked to know where he was going and he liked to get there. Her legs were moving faster, he couldn't help the sidelong glance to check the way her hips swayed in the tight denim. 'I'm not going too fast for you, am I?'

'Generally I prefer to take things a little easier, but I can keep up.' She shot him a look. 'I know you're busy.'

He answered at face value, pretending to ignore the little dig. 'Time is precious. Often I have my dictaphone with me and work on the walk.'

'A multitasking man?' she gushed. 'You amaze me.'

He grinned. 'Oh, I have a lot of talents.'

'I'm sure you do.'

The morning was bright and clear. The sun spread in sparkles on the water, the wind was non-existent and Daniel felt invigorated. He held the door for her at the café. She walked through it as if she'd never expected anything else. Matching him for putting on arrogant appearances.

'Coffee?'

'Thank you. Double, black, three sugars.'

He inclined his head and turned to the counter, his face cracking into the broadest grin as soon as he was out of her eyesight. Loose cannon. Utterly. He placed her order and his: triple shot, no sugar—nuclear amounts of caffeine to keep the tired bug at bay.

She sat in the front window of the café and stared out the window. Outwardly one might think she hadn't been aware of his approaching return, but Daniel was studying her hard and saw her shoulders tighten, saw the way she held her fingers tightly, and then he saw she wasn't staring out the window at all. She was staring at the reflection of him in the glass. He caught her gaze full on in the mirror-like pane. Gold meeting green. His pace slowed as he neared. Relentless observation, rising temperature.

When he set the cups down it shattered the moment. She turned away from the window and graced him with one of those sharp-edged smiles that assumed politeness. As if that searing stare had never happened.

He sat across from her.

She spoke. 'So what do you want to know?'

Everything. What she was thinking—about him especially. Raw attraction hung like an invisible fog between them. Did she see it too?

'Will you be able to pull it off?'

'Yes. I'm meeting with supply reps this morning and have called the bar crew in for a meeting this afternoon. I'll sort the DJs once I've spoken with the staff. The rest of the clean-up can be done by the team. Once we're restocked we'll be good to go. Then it's a matter of a little promo.'

'Promotion? You don't have much time.'

'The most important thing is word of mouth. If I can get the word into a few select ears, then we won't have any problem.'

'And can you?'

She smiled, slow and ultra-confident. 'Sure.'

CHAPTER FIVE

You constantly monitor progress

DANIEL'S office had a sweeping view across New Zealand's seat of power—the parliamentary buildings that stood across the road from the highest court in the country, and one of the finest law schools a quick step down the block. In that small radius, law was developed, made and upheld. And he felt right at home there. But today he could hardly wait to bust a move and head to the other side—where eclectic clothing stores lined up with funky cafés and hip clubs. Where the cool, cosmopolitan crowd from the film and fashion industries hung out—eating, drinking, dancing.

He didn't get there anywhere near as soon as he would have liked. Meetings dragged and unexpected developments trapped him in the office. It was late into the afternoon when he finally walked down the main street towards the club. The sign said 'closed' but the door stood ajar. He heard Lucy's voice as he climbed the stairs. He slowed so he could listen for a while before she was aware of his presence.

'What I want is professionalism. I know things have been slack since Lara left but all that changes right now. You saw what happened to the old manager this week. You'll be next if you don't lift your game. Uniform—black. Make the most of whatever assets you have but not too unsubtle—we're not a strip club. Look good but tidy. It's all about attitude—but by attitude I don't mean grumpy. We want to keep the customers happy, not turn them off with unsmiling, pouty looks. A little flirty is OK. This is a bar, people. Punters are here for a good time and a little action. Let's get them in the mood by getting them their drink quickly, and with flair. And quickly is the most important. At the end of the day we want to make money.'

Attitude, huh? Well, she'd know all about that. He smirked at the grumpy comment. He wished the staff had seen her at the pool this morning. He reached the top of the stairs and turned into the bar. Four workers were lined up behind the bar and in front of them stood a selection of drinks—shots, cocktails, a pint of beer. He saw all that in a nanosecond. He couldn't stop his focus closing in on *her.*

She stood on the punters' side of the bar, legs slightly spread, weight evenly distributed. Jeans again—emphasising the curves that had Daniel fantasising. By all appearances she'd been putting them through their paces. Either that or they were all about to get blind drunk together. 'Last example. Something for the drivers—lemon, lime and bitters.'

They moved at once getting glasses and mixing the drink.

The way she wore those jeans should be illegal. The combination of curvy and length was killing him. He wanted to peel the denim off her and wrap those tanned pins around his waist.

'Always ask if they would prefer to drink straight from the bottle or in a glass. Many women like to keep the bottle and the cap these days.'

His ears pricked. An interesting point given the case he was working on.

He looked over the staff. Two men, two women. All of them good-looking. The buffest guy dropped the glass and it smashed on the ground. He threw Lucy a look of horror. Daniel's lips twitched; she certainly had put the fear into him.

'Sorry, L-Lucy,' the buff guy stammered.

Lucy turned and saw he was watching. A sarcastic curl to her lips let him in on her secret laughter. He sent her a small smile back and tried to ignore the sweet feeling of conspiracy. He'd spent all his time so far verbally jousting with her and the idea of them sharing something other than conflict felt surprisingly good.

'Don't worry, Corey. It won't take you long to get to grips with it all.'

Who was she kidding? The guy could hardly string a sentence together. Daniel's hackles rose as Corey flashed Lucy a killer smile and she smiled right back.

'OK, people.' She turned and pointed to him. 'This is Daniel—he's the one who shut the place down last week and he won't hesitate to do it again, leaving us all penniless. So let's be nice to him and do a good job.'

Four pairs of big eyes warily looked him over. He stared back at them, poker-style. He'd spent too many days in court seeing off gang guys to feel much heat from a couple of beautiful bartenders. Lucy spoke again, giving more direction, and he took the opportunity to wander about and take in her changes. Every window was open and on the sills he saw some candles lit under oil burners. He walked over to one and sniffed. Yes. That was her—a warm, faintly exotic spice smell. He smelt it in her hair, her skin. He wondered if all of her was as delicately scented.

When he turned around the others were exiting, avoiding his eye. Lucy strolled over towards him.

He pulled his steamy thoughts in. 'Thanks for the warm introduction.'

'Someone has to be bad cop.'

'I'd have thought you'd enjoy that.'

'Oh, no. I'm always good.'

Sure she was.

'You really think that guy's capable of doing this job?' He nodded his head after Corey, who'd been last to leave after sweeping away what ominously looked like more than one dropped glass.

'Daniel, he can carry crates and he looks good.'

'It's all about looks?'

She rolled her eyes. 'Of course. Everybody likes to look at something beautiful.'

'Not everybody sees beauty in the same thing.'

'Don't worry. He's going to please a lot of our customers. And he can actually make a good cocktail.' She had a smile on her face that he didn't like. What was it about that guy that had her drooling? 'We get the customers in the bar, they have beautiful quick service and good music. If the vibe is good, they'll stay and pay.'

He nodded. It didn't seem too hard an equation. 'What are you planning to do with all those? Have your own party?' He gestured to the line-up of glasses.

'Unless you want them, they're going down the drain.' She tilted her chin—defiance in the stance. 'It's not a waste of stock, I needed to see what their skills were like.'

'I wasn't worried about that. You don't want one?'

She frowned. 'I don't drink.'

That surprised him. 'Ever?'

'Never at work. Never at a bar. I might have a glass of wine at home with people I trust.'

People she trusted? Why? He was about to ask when he heard someone's high heels clomping up the stairs at pace.

'Lucy, darling, sorry I'm late.'

Daniel turned and saw the tallest women he'd ever encountered come through the door at breakneck speed. He saw Lucy at an equal pace walk straight into her arms. Whoa. Then he saw her pull away and smile at the woman, and give her the whisper of a wink. 'Daniel, this is Sinead. She's the bouncer I was telling you about.'

She. Bouncer. OK. Great.

He looked the bouncer in the eye—almost. He was fractionally taller. Peripherally, he could see Lucy staring at him. Obviously she'd been hoping to shock him. Well, sorry, but he wasn't some sexist who thought that women couldn't work in any area. Although for a second there he'd wondered about their relationship. He didn't like Lucy walking into anyone else's arms—male or female…

What had he just thought? Daniel replayed the scene in his mind. Re-examined the feeling. *Territorial. Possessive.* That prehistoric man thing again.

For a moment he was stunned. Then he figured out the answer. A good twentieth century answer—it was no different from his usual approach. He'd sink deep into her softness and sate this full-on lust. He wanted her, he'd have her, and then he'd forget about her. Just because his want was extreme, didn't mean the rules had to be any different.

This train of thought delighted him so much he gave Sinead a huge smile. She blinked—so did Lucy.

'Fantastic, Sinead. I'm sure you'll be fabulous—Lucy wouldn't recommend you if you weren't.'

Lucy was picking her jaw up off the floor. Daniel nearly laughed aloud.

Sinead gave him a smile. She too met the beautiful barperson criteria. Daniel started to wonder if they were going to get done for being ugly-ist in their recruitment policy. At least six foot, with long blonde hair that was tied back in a pony-tail, Sinead was already outfitted in the regulation black—a slim, sleeveless top and tight black trousers. Add a mask and she'd be Catwoman.

'You do martial arts?'

'Of course.' She gave him a wide smile. 'I trained Lucy in the basics a few years ago. That's how we met.'

Why did Lucy want basic martial arts training? Why did she only drink with people she trusted? Daniel's curiosity escalated.

Lucy piped up, 'I've managed to convince her she needs an extra job on the weekends.'

'This is your first job as a bouncer?' He tried not to panic.

Sinead gave him a wide smile. 'Sure.'

He couldn't wait to get Lucy alone. He was going to kill her. OK, maybe he'd kiss her first.

Lucy was looking a tad uncomfortable. As she should. 'We have some things to work through, Daniel. Are you staying long?'

She was trying to dismiss him? 'No. I'm here for the afternoon. I'll go set up on the end of the bar there.'

With great satisfaction he saw the panic in her eyes. He pulled out his laptop again and laid out his files. He found this end of the bar comfortable. He could raise his head and survey the entire room. And it gave him prime view of the length of the bar—he could keep his eye right on her.

Lucy and Sinead sat at a table as far away as possible and spoke in low tones. Should he hassle her about cronyism? She'd clearly hired a friend. He pushed the thought away. If she was the best qualified for the job then fine. Frankly he had other things to be worried about—this case, for one. He just wanted the club open again and functioning as OK as possible. He wished Lara would get back a.s.a.p. so he could hand this sick puppy back to her and walk away from the woman occupying too much of his brain.

He focused on the books, finally able to concentrate knowing the wild one was in his line of sight. He lost himself in the law.

'You like watching women wrestle, Daniel?' She leaned over his shoulder and he could smell her spice. He jerked his head up and looked about the bar—Sinead appeared to have gone, leaving Lucy and him alone. His blood pumped a little faster.

'I like getting my work done in peace.'

She mocked him. 'Don't you ever muck about?'

'Not on my client's time.'

'Of course not. I was wrong—you should be good cop. Goody-good.'

'You really think I'm a boring square, don't you?'

'You're a lawyer. You couldn't be more straight.'

'Someone should hire you to do PR for my profession. Most of the population think we're crooked as.'

At that she smiled. 'You realise it's after six. Haven't you clocked off yet?'

'I work long hours.'

'Clearly.'

What did she mean by that? That he had no life? Hell, he spent half his evenings at some social event or other. And didn't have too much trouble finding dates to take with him. Pretty dates. Dates who wore designer, not…second-hand. He turned on his stool to face her, finding her enjoyably close. She made to step away but he stopped her by taking her wrist in his hand. She stilled completely. He liked the feel of her—as soft as he'd imagined. In his own time, in his own way, he'd show her exactly how un-boring he was. Soon. 'Have you never been in a job you love, Lucy?'

'Not for long.'

'And why is that?'

She shrugged, pulling her hand away. 'The love doesn't last long.'

He let her go—her words hitting a nerve. She'd given him a timely reminder. She was the epitome of everything he didn't like about women—unreliable. His desire, and the rest of him, cooled. 'Everything set for tomorrow?'

She nodded. 'It'll be just fine.'

'Good.' He pulled his papers towards him and started loading them back into his bag. 'I'm in meetings all day so I won't be here when you open up.'

'You're not going to be here?'

Disappointment touched her features and he schooled himself so satisfaction didn't touch his. 'I'll swing by later in the evening and see it's all OK.'

'But—'

'You can call me on my mobile if you need me.' He stared at her. She stared back. 'But you're not going to need me. Are you?'

Lucy swallowed. Yes, she needed him. But that had nothing to do with the bar. She liked him sitting there keeping her company. He hadn't noticed when Sinead had left—over an hour ago. She should have been sorting out the office some more but she'd found things to do out in the bar just so she could keep half an eye on him. The wrinkle in his brow when he was intently reading was undeniably cute. She liked the cut and thrust, the volley of alternates. His observance of her. His questioning. His look that suggested he felt as uncomfortable around her as she did around him.

No way was he her type. No way was she his.

But there was chemistry there. And they were circling around it like two wary wolves.

'I'll be fine.' She would too. The bar would open, drinks would be on hand, music would play and, hopefully, customers would arrive. But she had the fantasy of it being an all-out hit. Of bodies cramming the dance floor, steaming it up. Of her standing behind the bar, presiding over a couple of hundred happy clubbers out for a good time. And she wanted him to witness that—to see that she wasn't a flake. Wasn't 'just' a waitress who flitted from job to job. She'd run the place—not just keep it afloat but make it come alive. Prove her worth, not just to him, but to herself. Ordinarily she estimated her worth as pretty low. She was better at making mistakes than making much else out of life. But maybe she could really swing something here.

She'd spent half the morning out doing the rounds of the fashion establishments, hair salons and chic cafés. Dropping a word in here and there, leaving some flyers she'd knocked out. She knew everything, *everything* came down to word of mouth.

Lucy could do mouth. Get the beautiful women here, the right women, and the men would follow. So she'd made the calls, bluffed her way round without being too desperate-real-estate-agent sounding, and now all she could do was ensure the stage was furnished for the party people to play on.

True to his word he wasn't there when she opened up. And he still wasn't there when they were halfway through the shift. She told herself she didn't care because everything else was perfect. She couldn't quite believe it. Was she really making a success of something? Her? Lackadaisied Lucy? Sinead stood at the door downstairs in her black with her earpiece and microphone clipped on, her long blonde hair a river down her back—looking like every man's action-heroine fantasy come to life—attracting huge amounts of attention.

Corey was working the bar with her and so was Isabel. Both were in black as requested and their hair was perfect. Her own hair was as wayward as ever—crazy half-curls that were impossible to control. So she hadn't bothered. She'd just twisted it up out of the way. She too wore black—an A-line skirt to her knee, boots, mascara. But her top was scarlet—with black ribbon trim. No cleavage, not too tight, but definitely flattering. She and the others worked their respective parts of the bar relentlessly.

Lucy glanced over to the dance floor, amused by a gaggle of younger women dancing. Giggling together, they were having a fun time and try as they might the two guys standing at the edge of the bar couldn't maintain their conversation for more than ten seconds without their concentration being splintered by the sight.

Daniel might be concerned about fire and emergency regulations but there were other more insidious elements that could threaten the safety of the clientele. Lucy knew only too well the kind of dangers that could be snuck in by unscrupulous men.

She'd instructed Sinead to carefully ID-check any younger women, knowing how well some make-up and a dollop of confidence could add a few years onto a girl to take her from under age to entitled entry. She'd done it herself—one time too many—and she'd paid a price. One she didn't want anyone else to have to endure. So Sinead was downstairs, being tough.

But you didn't have to be under age to be at risk. So upstairs Lucy had told Corey to keep the window sills and ledges cleared, encouraging customers to keep their drinks with them—in their hands—at all times. She'd made sure the bathrooms were well lit. She'd locked the cleaning cupboard that was across the small hall from the lavatory doors. If she were going to be in charge for a longer stint she'd request a CCTV camera be installed in the vestibule. They might not be able to monitor it at all times, but they'd have recordings. And if anything did ever happen, they'd then have evidence.

That had been her problem—lack of evidence. She'd just been marked the troublesome teen that no one would believe. Worst of all, she didn't know what to believe herself. Her memory had been damaged by the chemical cocktail she hadn't known she'd had.

She shook off the unhappy reflections and breathed in the party atmosphere. Bad stuff wasn't going to happen here. She surveyed the scene once more. It was the success she'd dreamed of—almost. He hadn't been there to see it.

She checked her watch for the eightieth time that night and hid the frustration. She'd wanted him to see her success. She grumped—what did she care anyway? He was just a jerk in a suit who wouldn't know a good time if he fell over it. She, on the other hand, knew how to have fun in a club—by dancing. She shimmied along behind the bar, amusing herself by playing up to the punters. Smiling, chatting, never crossing the line, but encapsulating the sizzle vibe. They grooved to the music as they poured the drinks and kept the crowd coming back for refills. She laughed with Isabel over Corey's second broken glass of the night and went and stood over him, doing her Mistress Lucy dominating boss act that he fully played up to—knowing by now her bark was a whole lot worse than her bite.

When she turned back to the queue at her end of the bar Daniel was at the front—still in a suit, stubble darkening his jaw. Hot eyes burning into her, their golden lights gleaming. Her heart sped and her smile was huge. 'What'll you have? On the house.' She winked. Feeling friendly. Feeling like fun and frisk—and willing to take a risk.

'Just a quick beer. I'm not staying.'

She got a bottle of one of the best, fighting the disappointment. 'You should—it's going off.'

He looked around. 'Yep, you don't need my help.'

His sour demeanour annoyed her. 'Don't you like to have a good time, Daniel?'

'I prefer more intimate for my good times.'

'Do you? I prefer a party atmosphere.'

'Clearly.'

'Yeah. I like the thrill of being close in a big crowd but knowing you can't be as close as you really want.' She did too—the delight of suspense, the torture of wanting and having to wait. It made an evening fun.

'So you're a tease.' He sipped and added smartly, 'Figures.'

She experienced an almost uncontrollable urge to slap him. Completely foreign—even the most annoying customer had never irked her as much as he did. Did the guy not know anything about having fun? Fortunately for him a punter was impatiently waiting for a drink and she flounced away to serve him. Rushed to serve more, she didn't get to glance back. When she finally did, he was gone.

As she worked from one end of the bar to the other, sorting problems, getting Corey to clear tables, ensuring everyone got their ten minutes' break time, she fought harder and harder not to think about him. And failed completely. Why had he cleared off so quickly? Surely she'd seen the spark of desire in his face—in the pool this morning, in the café, in the bar tonight when he'd first caught her eye. She hadn't dreamt it. But then he'd been Mr Grump-a-rama. He preferred 'more intimate'? What did that mean?

Near-naked pictures from the pool raced through her mind again and she slammed the brakes on pronto. Did he feel the zing between them? Did he secretly love their sarcastic sparring too? God, he was hard to read. He just matched her for smart answer time and time again but really gave very little away. She wished she hadn't seen him in little more than a towel. Who would have thought that such a body could lie under that straight white shirt and tie? He wore a suit well—very well.

He wore nothing better.

She shook her head and concentrated on serving up the last few drinks, instructing the DJ to switch to mellow tunes that would send out the home-to-bed vibe. After the last of the customers cleared, she and the others did a quick tidy. The rest would be done by the cleaner in the morning. Lucy turned the music down and printed out data from the computer.

Sinead paused on her way out. 'You sure you're OK being left alone in here?'

'So long as you lock the door on your way out I'm fine.' Lucy winked. 'And I know a few moves, remember?'

She listened to Sinead clomp down the stairs and heard the satisfying click of the door below. Then she slumped in a chair in relief. She'd done it and done it well. And it had been such fun—until Daniel had come and gone again. Her happy mood slipped.

Mad with herself for being so down over *him*, she went to her bag and rummaged through her CD file. Finding the one she was after, she loaded it into the machine and turned it up loud. The early hours of the morning were still hot and she opened a couple of the windows wider, lit an oil burner and put it on one of the centre tables to help get rid of the smell of booze and the perfumes of a hundred bodies. Then she danced—with the freedom she always had when the music was up loud and she was alone.

* * *

Daniel gently shook his half-full glass as he sat on his deck in the warm breeze and looked at the city lights reflected on the water. He wasn't sleepy. Not even a little bit. The club would be closed now. She'd have gone home for the night. He realised he didn't even know where her home was. Her CV only had her mobile phone number as her contact. He toyed with the idea of texting her—to make sure the place was locked up tight.

His phone buzzed—was it thought transference? He answered, body seizing as a female voice said hello. Then his brain clicked on.

'Hi, Lara.' Oh.

'Is everything at the club OK?'

'Yeah, it's fine.'

'You get someone good?'

'Yeah.' Try stunning. Try teasing. Try truly aggravating.

'Many there?'

'A few.' Honestly he couldn't really say. His eyes had been on her from the moment he'd walked in. She hadn't noticed him. He'd had the 'pleasure' of watching her flirt with buff guy before he'd made his way to her end of the bar. She'd been right about the attitude and the look—although she hadn't been head-to-foot black, her top a slash of scarlet. Trust Lucy to break her own uniform rule. He remembered Lara waiting on the end of the call. 'Quite a few actually. Lots.'

'Are you OK? You sound distanced.'

'Must be the line.' They made an impressive line-up of bar staff—buff guy, the petite brunette and the tall, tanned curvy one with the brilliant smile. She'd smiled her way through serving her customers and they'd all smiled back. Every one. Even the women. So how come he got it so infrequently? It was as if she'd taken one look at him, decided he was an arrogant jerk and been point-scoring ever since.

'I'm not sure when I'll be back.' Lara didn't sound remotely sorry.

'That's OK. I can handle it until you do.' But could he handle his lust for Lucy? Little Miss Smart Mouth—openly antagonistic because she thought he was some stuffed shirt. But her eyes had gone smoky at moments when they'd been physically close—there were sparks there. He wanted to blow on them, and then stamp them out.

'Thanks, Daniel. I knew you wouldn't let me down.'

'No problem.'

He pressed the end button and set his glass down with a snap. If he was going to be awake at this time he might as well be working on his case notes. He glanced at the box on the floor by his feet. No chance. Instead he stood. A walk would help. Clear the mind and make him tired so he'd sleep. He'd walk through town, past the club, make sure it was all shut up and secure.

There were a few stragglers still on the road but it was largely quiet, peaceful and warm. Despite the couple of mouthfuls of whiskey he'd had he was stone-cold sober. As he neared the club he started to walk that little bit faster—he could hear music. Worse than that, he could hear *country* music. Well past closing. He got to the door—it was locked and the stairwell light was off. He walked into the middle of the road so he could see up to the windows and into them a little—they were wide open and there was a light on inside. What the hell was going on? Was she staging some sort of lock-in? The music was appalling. Had she turned the place into a line-dancing school? Either way it was being shut down now.

He shouldn't have hired her. Never should have done it. He'd been bamboozled by a beautiful body and eyes that begged for him to believe in her.

Idiot.

He pulled the keys out of his pocket and inserted them in the lock. She was about to be sacked.

CHAPTER SIX

It is essential for you to try things with your own hands

LUCY was whirling round the floor, arms outstretched, when she heard it. Heavy footsteps on the stairs. Inside. Coming up. Fast. She stopped still. Brain spinning. She dashed for the bar and got behind it. Then cursed herself for her stupidity. If he was after cash he'd come straight for the till. She thought about her mobile phone—in her bag in the back room. Useless. Fear slashed through her but she refused to freeze. She had to fight.

Her mind flickered, eyes hunting for a weapon. Glasses, bottles—weapons which would be used against her. Then she saw it—the postmix—the drink dispenser. She could squirt soda at the intruder and dash for the fire alarm with the seconds that bought her. She lifted the nozzle from its rung and stood square on to the door just as it opened and she saw the manly figure outlined—tall, broad, familiar. Body achingly familiar.

'What the hell are you doing?' they shouted simultaneously.

Lucy swore as he advanced and she saw it truly was him. Her heart didn't know whether to speed up, slow or stop altogether.

'You gave me one hell of a fright.' She couldn't mute the remains of high-strung panic. Snatching quick, full breaths, she tried to calm. The relief washing through her was as effective at shutting off her brain functionality as the fear had been moments before.

What was he doing here? Especially looking like that? Angry, dishevelled and so, so hot. He still wore his suit but the jacket and tie were gone now. It was just his white shirt, unbuttoned at the neck, tails escaping his trousers, and even rougher stubble on his jaw.

'Well, what are you doing? You should be home by now and this place should be shut up.'

'Don't worry, I'm not going to get your precious licence revoked.'

'So what about the licence? It's dangerous for you to be here alone at this time. You should leave when the others do and go home in a cab.'

'I was sorting the paperwork.'

'Do it tomorrow. With music like that Noise Control will be here any moment.'

'It's not that loud.'

'No, but it is truly awful.'

'Don't you like country?'

'Hell, no.' His glare softened. 'Just what were you planning on doing with that?' He nodded towards her hands.

She remembered she still held the postmix. Devilish temptation called. Not water—not enough power. Cola would stain and the taste brought back horrible memories. It would have to be lemonade. Her fingers flexed. Her hands raised to aim.

He saw the movement. His eyes narrowed. His mouth opened.

Before sound emerged, she pressed the button. Frothy lemonade squirted out, hitting him square on the chest. His shirt was soaked in seconds. He stood still, not giving any clue to his reaction. The liquid raced, leaving a translucent path down his chest, fitting the material to him like second skin.

She stared. 'Maybe you should revisit the strip-club idea.' She cleared her throat. 'Or at least instigate a wet-tee-shirt night. Or wet business shirt.' She couldn't stop the huge smile spreading across her features, the burgeoning glow of amusement, the flame of desire, the illicit thrill that she got from his unreadable expression. How was Mr Cool Collected Type A going to handle this?

She lifted the nozzle again.

He spoke. 'You. Dare.'

Goose-bumps peppered her skin, but her smile still grew. She got him in the hair and face this time.

And then he moved. Faster than she'd thought possible for such a big guy. He took three paces and vaulted over the bar to where she stood. In a split second he had the postmix out of her hand and held it firm in his and she was pinioned to his side by his spare arm.

She squirmed. He squeezed—pulling her even closer.

'You know you're trouble with a capital T.' He waved the nozzle at her. 'You're about to get really wet.'

It must have been his proximity that caused her to do it. She looked at the broad chest against her, wanting to taste the trickling bubbles of soda. She wanted to taste him. She breathed in his male musky scent. The hit kicked her inner vixen to life. She replied, a slow, sassy drawl.

'I already am.'

She lifted her lashes and let the lust out. Unthinking, uncaring. Just wanting the moment. *Now.*

He stood stock-still, body rigid. His gaze slowly left hers and lowered, to her lips and down—to her perfectly dry top. Then he looked back up—and to her delight the gold had flamed into life.

His arm pulled her even tighter to him and she sucked in a breath as her body flared against the hard feel of his.

'Yes.' She was close enough to feel his breath on her skin, to see the stubble on his jaw—almost close enough to flick her tongue out to taste him. She couldn't control it. Her tongue touched the tip of her own lip—a tiny, flickering movement.

He tossed the postmix away. She heard it clatter on the bar

and then that sense shut down as his other arm closed around her. She became aware only of the feel of him. Close, so close. His gaze had fixed on her mouth and she lifted it as he brought his down slowly.

Their bodies touched, chest to chest, abdomen, hip, thighs and finally lips. Sealing them from top to toe. The kiss was slow. Soft. Simple. But it heralded complications of seismic proportions. From the second his mouth pressed on hers it was all over. There was no way she wasn't taking this to completion—him to completion—and her.

He lifted his head a whisker and the pulse throbbing in her lips forced her to part them. Immediately he was back and the soft, slow kiss resumed.

He had patience, able to take time for careful consideration.

She didn't.

She wanted it all. Right now.

So she slipped her hands up between her and him, wanting to unfasten the buttons of his wet shirt. But found she couldn't. The wet made the material hard to manoeuvre. So she just pulled, heard the rip, then felt the warmth. Fingertips touching the smooth skin that sheathed hard muscle.

She felt her moan rather than heard it. Loved it when he yanked her that little bit closer in reply. Soft became stronger. His hands lifted and worked into her hair, holding it tight at the roots. He took a step forward, forcing her back against the bar.

She ran her hands across the top of his chest, loving the heated strength. His hands massaged in her hair, fingers working through its length. Then one came to cup her jaw, to hold her as his kisses grew in intensity and her response grew more fevered.

She'd never imagined he'd kiss like this. That Mr In Control could have her so out of control in just a few minutes. She felt the shift deep inside. Her body readying, ripening. Wanting it all.

He seemed to sense it. His hands moved from her hair and face to her waist where they gripped and he lifted her up to seat her on the bar. He lifted his head and looked at her while his hands went to her knees—pushing them apart so he could stand between them. Then he reached round her back again and slid her forward on the bar so she perched right on the edge of it—so her open body was pressed against his. Unhesitatingly she wound her legs around his waist. This was what she'd wanted from the first moment she'd clapped eyes on him. Lust at first sight. Suit be damned.

The kisses resumed—deep, his tongue searching, conquering. And she ran her hands over his shoulders, pulling at the remnants of the wet shirt, pulling it down his arms until he shook it free, flinging it over the bar. She took a second to study the bronzed torso before her. Still damp, super hot. Defined muscles bunched, taut nipples tempted her, but before she could do as she wanted and lean in to taste he was pushing her skirt up to bare her thighs. His fingers trailed fire, teasing, striking at her need. His smile grew wicked at her sharp inhalation of breath. He undid the button at the back. This guy might seem to be square but he was by no means inexperienced in the art of undressing a woman. Maybe he was more of a player than she'd realised. Maybe it wasn't all work. Right now she couldn't care less. In fact it was cause for celebration; the sooner they were both free of fabric, the happier she'd be. He unzipped the skirt and, bunching it in his hands, slipped it up, scooping her top at the same time and taking both off over her head. She raised her arms to help. Then she was in panties, bra and cowgirl boots. His hands smoothed over her thighs, rubbing ever upwards while his head bent to kiss soft, hot kisses from her collar-bones to her peaking breasts. She gasped, things were happening fast now—her body melting, desperate for him, but her brain couldn't keep up. She needed to keep some semblance of control—of protection.

'You know you're still not my type.' It sounded so school-girl but it was the best she could come up with under pressing circumstances.

'And you're not mine, but we're doing this regardless.'

Oh, yes.

Her panties were wetter than his shirt had been and she didn't have the postmix to blame. The sense of urgency increased.

His hands slipped the bra straps from her shoulders and unclasped the back of it. He stared at her bared breasts. She could see the flush in his face.

'Condom?' One word. Primitive male.

'Bathroom.' She panted. 'Dispenser.'

He scooped her off the bar and she tightened her legs round his waist, kissing him. He headed in the direction of the toilets.

She pulled back. 'Coin-operated.'

He swore and then swiftly headed to the back of the bar. His skill at walking while carrying and kissing her was impressive.

He punched at the cash register and took coins from the compartments.

'Discrepancies in the till,' she muttered as she lifted her head from nuzzling his warm, rough jaw.

'I'll replace it later.'

'That's what they all say.' She felt his chuckle and giggled aloud herself.

He hoisted her higher so he could suck her nipples as he walked through the bar to the restrooms. Lucy was thankful she'd cleared the chairs from the floor space—ample room to weave over the floor in abandon.

They made it to the bathroom. He barged through the door and pulled up next to the vending machine.

She looked at him. He was unable to operate the machine while holding her.

'I'm not letting you go.' He grinned. 'I can feel that wet heat through your panties on my stomach and it's a sensation I'm not willing to give up yet.'

She twisted round to get the coins from him and dropped them in the slot. 'Preference?'

'You choose.'

He was making any kind of decision impossible, the way he was nipping at her breast. Teasing. She pressed the first button and with satisfaction pulled the package from the hold, waving it in victory above her head. He rewarded her with a kiss even hotter than before.

She had to break it, tipping her head, letting her hair tumble down her back, winding her arms tighter round his neck, enjoying the movement of his hard abs against her as he walked.

He strode back through to the bar and with single-minded purpose went to the far end of the room and laid her on the pool table. He kicked off his shoes and his trousers slipped from his waist. He stretched forward onto the table. His shoulders broad, his arms long and muscular as they braced over her. She lay back, propped on her elbows, delighting in the hunger she saw in his face as he skimmed down her body, stopping at her centre.

He pressed his open mouth to the crotch of her panties. Her hips jerked. Her hands fisted. Her squeal instant. Involuntary. Ecstatic.

He looked up to her and spoke, the old challenge back in his eyes. 'I hope I'm not going too fast for you?'

She looked down at him, his handsome face between her spread thighs, his near-naked body primed and poised. She licked her lips and drawled right back at him. 'I think I can keep up.'

Fact was he wasn't going fast enough. Would he just get her panties off! He bent to her again but she couldn't stand it. The sensation of his mouth on her, his tongue tasting, but that scrap of silk in the way. She went to rectify it herself, her hands going to the elastic waistband, tugging it down, but his hands covered hers, stopping her actions.

He looked up at her. 'I like to unwrap my presents slowly, savour each part as it's revealed.'

'I like to rip the paper off and play with the toy right away.'

'This isn't going to be over in thirty seconds, Lucy. This isn't one toy that you're going to play with, break and forget about in five minutes.'

Their eyes met in deadlock.

'You think?' She'd better forget about him in five minutes. This was so not a good idea but, hell, too late now.

'I know.'

His confidence simultaneously annoyed and excited her. 'Prove it.'

He threw his head back and laughed. 'I don't need to prove it, Trouble. I only have to touch you like this and I know.' He slid a finger under the leg of her panties and stroked—just the once. She clamped her jaw to stop the moan escaping.

'See?' His finger left her panties again. 'Now where was I?' He looked down again. 'Unwrapping.'

He ran his tongue along the edge of her panties. Her stomach muscles contracted. His hands slid up her torso to toy with her breasts again. It was then she realised Daniel might not play as fair as he ought. He was deliberately setting out to torment her.

That thought gave her the licence to abandon herself completely. Give over to his way of doing things. Let him have this moment. She'd have her turn shortly. Fine. That wasn't so difficult. So she let go, her hips moving as she wanted, rising to meet his kisses, enabling him to remove her panties inch by painfully slow inch. She let her arms float in the air as he buried his face into her—learning her.

When his tongue flicked against her, her whole body tensed. His rhythm increased. Oh, yes. She'd take it now. Moments from climax, she called to him. 'Oh, yes. Yes!'

Then suddenly he slowed, right when she wanted it fast to take her that last inch to ecstasy.

And while it was wildly frustrating it was also incredibly intense, ratcheting up her excitement to a level she hadn't known was possible. Then he began to speed up again.

She smiled as she sighed. This time.

But just as she neared he slowed again—right down. Torturous.

'Daniel.'

He lifted his head and gave her a wicked look. 'I'm not boring you now, am I?'

She threw him a look of utter venom and he threw back his head and laughed. Then the smile turned sinful again and he bent to tease her some more.

She felt even more excited by the way he'd suddenly become so playful, provocative, passionate. But it was time for her to take charge. Heat flooded through her, as did a surge of female strength. She sat up, slipping her hips back from him. He looked up.

'Come here.'

He pulled up onto the pool table, stretching out beside her.

She ran a forceful arm from his shoulder to belly. 'Don't think you can mess with me, Daniel.'

'Why? What are you going to do about it?'

Make him pay. He'd said she was a tease, although it seemed to her that the boot was on the other foot—his. Well, she could give as good as she got.

She pushed his chest so he lay down and moved to straddle him. Then she slid up onto his belly so his erection didn't press against her—she knew her own limitations and getting too close to that would be game over. She leant over him, watching as his pupils widened the nearer her breasts got. She knew he liked them, had seen him sneaking quick peeks at them from the moment they'd first met. The way he'd been burying his face in them when she'd been getting the condom had been a bit of a give-away too. She brushed her nipples against his open mouth. Shivered as he expertly caught one in his mouth. She let him tease a little before pulling back. He was going to be the one in trouble.

She bent, trailing kisses down his chest, wanting to get to know him—all of him. But he grabbed her hair, pulling her away from him. Took her by the shoulders and lifted her to lie beside him. Then he rolled onto her, trapped her. She was happy to be caught. He held her gaze. 'What do you want from me?'

'Everything you have to offer.' Flippant but at the same time, for once in her life, totally honest.

'And what do I get in return?'

'The same.' She ran her hand across his shoulders, the heady passion making her reveal more than she intended. 'You have such a beautiful body.'

'So it's my body you want. Not my mind?'

She frowned. 'I think we should leave our minds out of it.' She reached up to touch him again, breathe in his scent. 'No thoughts. No analysis…'

'No regrets.' He kissed her. 'Just tonight. Just once.'

He'd told her in the temp agency he didn't do commitment. Nor did she—not with him. Neither of them would ever commit to their polar opposite.

She kissed her acquiescence. Once was just fine—so long as it was *right now.*

He lifted his head and muttered, 'Where's the condom?'

She found it near the top right-hand pocket of the pool table. She grabbed it, pausing as she saw he lay in the rectangle of light from the streetlights outside. Stretched out like some superb sex god—relaxed but ready for action.

He'd slipped his boxers off while she'd retrieved the packet so she saw him utterly naked for the first time.

She drew in another sharp breath. Thank God he'd had the towel around him at the pool the other day—if he'd been in swimwear designed to show off *that* bulge she'd have been hard pressed not to have pounced sooner. As it was she was about to do something stupid but it was far, far too late. Her brain was rendered inoperable. All she wanted was him. Her hands shook.

'Everything OK?'

'Oh, yes.' She glanced down again. 'Fine.'

'Sure?'

'Uh-huh.' She couldn't get the packet open, her fingers were so clumsy.

All she wanted was for him to be inside her. *Now, now, now.* She wanted to explore him.

He chuckled. 'Let me do that.'

He had it open in a second and rolled it on—she drank in every detail as he did so. Oh. Yes.

He looked up at her. Reached a hand out to caress the side of her cheek and draw her close for another blistering kiss. How could he affect her like this? How could she have lost all defences just like that?

He gently pushed her back, taking control, setting up their position. A good thing seeing how she'd seemed to have lost all capability. He kissed down the length of her again, his hands teased as her body trembled. She was at the point of losing it. She wound her arms around him, pulled at him to come back up her, to lie on her, to push that magnificent penis in where it belonged. Her breathing was audible—half moans, almost entreaties. Uncaring of how desperate she sounded, she called to him. There was no room for a cool, sarcastic veneer here. The only thing in her mind and body was want. He moved to answer her.

She parted her legs, wriggled her hips, positioning them to cradle his. She nipped at his lips. 'Don't even think about stopping now.'

'No,' he agreed, his mouth plundering hers once more. She stilled, waiting for the moment. He looked to her face, expression hot, as he read her soul in the moment they met.

She cried out, her head tipping back, closing her eyes from his intensity—only able to cope with the feel of him, not the vision as well…not yet. That was too much, too overwhelming. Once, twice, he stroked and then it hit. The tornado of excitement he'd been brewing in her all evening—all week. Her legs and arms tautened, tensing hard enough to cause muscle-burn, and her fingers caught in his hair, pulling, twisting as unbearable pleasure wrenched through her.

The screams were pure instinct, an animal response to the experience of utter joy.

He paused while her body shook out the sensations. Twisting. Trembling.

Finally she opened her eyes and took in his look of arrogant satisfaction. She felt the confidence in the way his arms encircled her. The sight of such masculine control brought her feminine fighter to the fore.

He was enjoying himself, oh, yes. But that wasn't enough for her. She wanted him to lose it. As she just had. And she wanted to be the one to make him. She gulped in a hit of oxygen and smiled. Then she worked her muscles. She saw his eyes widen. Worked them harder—her smile growing as she felt the hiss of air forced from his lungs. Lifting her head to twirl her tongue around his nipple, she took a tight butt cheek in each hand and pressed him closer. He wasn't the only one who could satisfy.

She felt his power surge as the game went up another level. Felt him rally to challenge right back and she blindly laughed—a low, husky laugh that he echoed. And then she kissed him, her mouth caressing every available inch of skin within her reach as she trailed her hands over him, gently at first, then not so gentle, and then with authority, sweeping down his back, demanding he keep time with the rhythm of her body.

His hands cupped her bottom, holding her to him, tighter as he took charge again. She clasped him close. All thought gone. All reason vanished. Only indescribable feelings that finally focused into rapture when she heard his cry and felt his control break.

CHAPTER SEVEN

Objective feedback is always helpful

SHE woke with a start. The chill of pre-dawn hit her together with confusion. For a split second she couldn't think, couldn't remember where she was, who she was with. All she sensed was the smell of stale beer and the stifling weight of someone on her. Terror-struck, she flinched and pushed in panic. Memories—old and new—rushed back.

In the bar. Daniel. She was with Daniel. Real. Not the fuzzy stranger who invaded her sleep and gave her nightmares. She sucked in a deep breath and relaxed, safe. But then she realised she must have fallen asleep.

At her movement he jerked his head up. 'What?' He blinked, looking into her eyes. For a moment the same confusion flashed across his face. Then he closed it down, shuttering his expression, and their eyes locked, neither giving anything away.

For once she won the duel. He looked away, a small frown pleating his brow.

She wriggled, wanting to escape the intimacy. He moved so she could sit up. She was amazed at her lapse. She never slept with a lover. Had sex, sure, but never allowed herself to lose consciousness—that was too intimate, too vulnerable. Lucy didn't do vulnerability. She refused to put herself in the position of giving someone else control over her heart, mind or body.

The scary thing was, she'd almost given Daniel exactly that. How much had she given away just now? Not just her body. Her heart was putting itself on a plate this very minute. She took it straight back to the fridge.

'You're getting cold?' He clipped out the words as he moved away from her. 'I'm sorry, I fell asleep.'

She flinched. She wasn't the only one going cold; he was as icy as the moment she'd first met him—remote, detached, disapproving. Her whole body hit sub-zero temperatures. She didn't know why his emotional detachment bothered her. He'd said once only. She already knew he didn't do commitment. Hell, *she* didn't do commitment—not at this point in her life. So much for no regrets. He looked as if he was itching to get out of here. Definitely not wanting to talk about it. Well, she wasn't going to do a cringesome cling-on act. She needed to save face and re-establish a protective layer. She'd never expected him to be so potent, so passionate. Time to back-pedal—fast. She hid behind the curtain of her hair. 'Well, I guess we got that out of the way.'

'Out of the way?'

She flicked her hair back and bluffed indifference. 'Yeah, scratched the itch. Quenched the curiosity.'

'Curiosity?'

'Mmm hmm.' She swung her legs off the pool table. Oh, man, she was still wearing her boots.

His hand caught her arm and he turned her to face him. 'What exactly are you saying, Ms Delaney?'

'I'm saying, Mr Graydon, that that was fun.'

'Fun?' He stared at her, but she couldn't figure a thing from the lights reflected in his eyes.

'Sure. It was OK. But we won't be doing it again.'

'We won't.'

She shook her head. 'Too messy.'

He glanced at the felt of the pool table. She followed suit and felt her cheeks fill with blood. Her wet and his sweat marked it. Hell. She'd have to hand in her notice immediately. Frustration flooded through her. She'd just done this job so well. For the first time she'd actually aced something. Now she'd stuffed it by sleeping with her Type A boss who'd just been waiting for her to trip up. Any other gig and she'd be on the road, not willing to put up with that kind of pressure.

The frustration turned into fight. She was tired of starting over. She'd had her first taste of success and she wanted another. She wanted to show *him* three times over. Besides, she needed the cash.

Even more reason to blow the whistle on this little interlude. She'd do it as coolly as she could and ignore the way she was quaking inside. Block out that secretly she wanted more. No vulnerability allowed—not around Mr Ice.

'Look, Daniel. I'm working for you. I was curious. It was nice but we're done. Let's go back to our business relationship, shall we? I'm sorry. Blame it on the heat of the night—the success of the relaunch went to my head.'

His eyes didn't leave her face the entire time she spoke. She curled her fingers into fists and tried to ignore his superb nudity.

'And caused you to ravish me.'

'Ravish *you?*' He'd done the ravishing. She sure felt like she'd been ravished. He'd broken down defences she'd been sure were insurmountable. But he didn't know that and, even if he did, if his current expression was anything to go by, he didn't care.

'I wasn't the one who ripped the buttons off this shirt.' His muscles flexed across his back as he bent to retrieve it.

OK, so she'd been eager to get it started.

'I wasn't the one who couldn't open the condom packet because of having the shakes so bad.'

There was nothing she could say to that so she went for the silent, avoid-eye-contact approach.

He stepped back towards her as she sat on the edge of the table. 'I wasn't the one screaming the house down.'

Now that was below the belt. She looked away from the rippling muscles on show and swallowed back the desire. Let icy anger trickle in.

'Come on. You were all over me.'

Well, of course she was. He was a god. He had the body of an Olympian and the technique of a master. She'd been weak just by looking and conquered with the first kiss. She had to pull back now because he was never going to be reciprocating her kind of stupidity. *Once only. No analysis.*

He took her silence in the way she intended. 'Never again?'

She shook her head.

'We've satisfied your curiosity and once was enough?'

She nodded.

He took another step forward and ran his finger from her neck to her breast—and she couldn't control the tremor. 'How long has it been?'

Oh, so he thought that was relevant? She refused to look at him. Maybe it was. Maybe that was why she felt so in danger of emotional investment. Honestly, she'd been without for so long even she could hardly remember.

'That long, huh?' A little laugh escaped him—whisker of humanity. That it was amusement at her expense made her mad. He ran his finger over her tightly shut lips, teasing them. 'You know, you're not so good with manners, Lucy. Didn't anyone ever teach you to mind your "p"s and "q"s?'

She threw him a vile look. His smile faded and the mask of indifference that took its place was much better than hers had been—probably because it was genuine.

'So we haven't broken through your male-bravado layer. Maybe we never will. Whatever.'

He strolled from the pool table with casual ease. 'Come on, let's go.' He collected his scattered clothing along the way.

She stood up and stared after him. Deflated. Well, she'd done it. Had she been hoping for more of an argument from him? Or wanting him to say, 'No, babe, that was fantastic, we've got to do it again'? At least offer some clue to his thoughts? He was shut up tighter than a twenty-year-old jar of pickled peppers. She watched as he pulled on his boxers, then felt irritated as a feeling of loss hit her when his body was hidden from her again.

He pulled on the trousers but held his sodden shirt in his hand. 'We'll share a cab.'

Panic surged as a new threat occurred to her. 'No, that's OK. I can walk.'

'No. It's late. You're tired.'

'It's almost light out. I'll be fine.'

'No argument. Get your jacket.' Now he was doing the gentleman act? Terrible timing.

'No, Daniel, I'm fine.'

'OK, I'll get it for you.'

'Daniel!'

He didn't listen. She hurried after him, stress giving her speed. She knew the job would be over the minute he saw her stuff there. He walked straight into the back room. Stopped. Saw her pack and violin case. Saw her sleeping bag on the two-seater sofa—unrolled with her sweatshirt rolled into a makeshift pillow at the head. He stared at it, then at her. 'What the hell is going on?'

She didn't have any clothes on—save her cowgirl boots. She didn't have a home to go to. She'd just slept with her boss and then rejected him. She was in such a mess. It was so typical. She could always count on her innate ability to stuff things up.

'What's your address, Lucy?'

'Daniel, I—'

'Street address. Now.'

Would he give her a second to answer? Riled, she spat, 'I'm not in a flat at the moment. I got to Wellington on Monday. I've been in a hostel but can't stand sleeping in a room full of strangers. I struggle to sleep as it is.'

'Insomnia?'

She nodded. 'Terrible.'

'Another thing we have in common.' He might be acknowledging something they shared, but he sounded arctic.

She smiled in empathy, hoping it would help her case.

The glacier refused to melt. Not even a drop. 'We should quit while we're ahead.'

OK, so the empathy bid failed. She turned back to bolshy. 'I thought I'd crash here until I set up a flat.'

'You thought wrong. You can't sleep here.'

'It's only for a night or two, Daniel.' Was he familiar with the concept of leeway?

'This building is zoned commercial, not residential.'

Clearly not. 'Rules and regulations, huh, Daniel?'

Green eyes met gold. His were flaming again—but not with hot lust. Now it was all cold anger. 'You are not sleeping here, Lucy.'

Fine. She marched into the room beside him and bent—starting to roll her sleeping bag.

'Lucy.'

If iron will could speak, it would sound like Daniel.

'What?' She snapped the question, while still stuffing her sleeping bag into its carrier.

'Might I suggest you put some clothes on?'

She stopped then, suddenly aware of how she must look to him standing behind her. Naked. Cowgirl boots. Bending over. 'Sure.'

She marched out of the room and back to the bar, pulling on her top and skirt—not bothering with either bra or panties. When she got back to the room, less than a minute later, he'd finished packing away her sleeping bag. Her violin case was at his feet and he carried her pack on one shoulder. He held her jacket out to her.

'Come on.'

She didn't take it. 'What do you mean come on?'

'You're coming home with me.'

'In your dreams.'

'Right home. Right now.'

She stared at him. Stunned at his words.

'I'm not kidding, Lucy. I have a perfectly good spare bedroom. It is almost six in the morning. I have a load of work to do later and I am not going to spend hours standing here arguing with you. You won't have to sleep with strangers. And certainly not me, as you've made it clear you couldn't think of anything worse. Let's move on.'

For once in her life Lucy was struck speechless. He was so cool about it. He wore that remote expression that had her wanting to leap up and do something drastic to get his attention again. Hot attention. But he'd come over all clinical.

The warm air of the early morning contrasted sharply with the chilly silence in which they walked along the bay to his apartment. He'd insisted on carrying her pack. She'd insisted on carrying her violin. There was where the conversation ended.

His apartment was as swanky as she'd expected. Floor-to-ceiling glass windows gave splendid harbour views. Stylish, minimalist, obviously designer-done, the whole place screamed suited bachelor—one who spent too many hours at work. He showed her to her room. Big bed, white spread. She walked away from it. 'Thank you.' She hoped to dismiss him immediately.

His response was even cooler. 'No problem. Stay as long as you like.'

She thought about taking him up on that—a good six months? That would serve him right. But then she turned and saw him there in suit trousers and no shirt and desire rose again—together with the panic. 'It'll be a couple of nights tops.'

He shrugged. 'There's an *en suite* through that door,' and he left the room.

She breathed out and went straight to the bathroom. It was a wet room—a large shower space and central drain. Multi shower jets pointed at her. It was too good to ignore.

She stripped off, savoured the scent of Daniel on her skin and quickly turned the water on hot.

Lucy didn't sleep a wink but made a show of staying in her room until well after midday. She waited for the muffled sounds to disappear and then finally she ventured out. Opened her door to peek and listen again. Silence. She walked out and, following the hall, found the main living area, taking her time to actually notice the surroundings this time. Beautifully decorated—perfect paintwork, the furniture expensive and comfortable looking, but the whole place was so, so…boring was the only word for it. The entire apartment could be a display in a posh furniture store. She looked about for some element of personality. Something to tell her a little more about Daniel. But there was nothing. She figured that told her as much as anything.

The colours were warm—chocolate blended with neutrals and greys. Totally tasteful. The kitchen showed no sign of life—no notice board with scrawled numbers, no pile of paperwork on the desk in the corner. Magnificently minimalist.

Lucy liked maximalist. Colour and chaos and life.

Even his bookcases were unnaturally neat—stacked with big hardback books that looked as if they'd take a lifetime to read. Then she found it. One solitary photograph framed in a dark wooden frame standing in place of some books in one of the bookcases lining the wall opposite the windows. She picked it up.

Daniel in full legal regalia—wig and gown, standing next to an older man also in wig and gown. It had to be his father. Had to be. They had the same jaw, same nose, Daniel stood only an inch or two taller, the old and the new. The similarities were striking—except for the eyes. His father's were brown—plain brown. But Daniel's were that wild tawny colour, with those amber lights hinting at the warmth and passion and humour that he seemed so determined to hide. In the photo his expression was serious, veiled. All remote austerity again—just like this apartment. She frowned.

Daniel watched her, screened behind the fine light curtain half drawn across the open balcony doorway. She was taking her time over that photo. He stood, his discomfort at having her in his apartment finally impelling him to move. Daniel didn't entertain here. He far preferred to stay at his lover's place so he could leave early in the morning and avoid any moments of intimacy over breakfast—moments that might lead the lady to think a relationship may be in the offing. Daniel didn't do relationships.

But Lucy wasn't such a lover. They'd had sex but that was it. Supposedly. He'd said himself it would only be the once. But he had to admit he'd really, really enjoyed it. She'd been wild. And his body had revelled in the heat and softness of hers.

He felt keyed up—as he had all night, knowing she was under his roof. For a moment there, after they'd had sex, he'd slept as comfortably as if he were in a bed made with pure cotton sheets and soft coverings, not on top of an old scarred pool table with scratchy felt.

Knowing that had happened made him tense, wary, and more determined to push her away than pull her close. Despite his basic instinct telling him to have her again. Right now his muscles and his mind were strung out from warring with each other, and with analysing why she'd been pushing too—away.

'Seen enough?'

She jumped a clear foot. Stared as he walked in from the balcony. 'I thought you weren't here.'

'Clearly.' He pointedly looked at the picture still in her hand.

But it seemed she had no qualms about her inquisitiveness. 'This your dad?'

He nodded. Regular Sherlock Holmes, she was.

'Did your mum take the photo?'

He froze, blood colder than a snake's. 'No.'

'Is it your graduation?'

So she'd moved on from the family questions. Excellent. 'Admission to the Bar.' Having secured his law degree, he'd then had to take some professional papers to be able to practice law. This was the formal presentation of that achievement.

'Your mum wasn't there?'

Damn. 'She was there.' Second to back row. She'd been late and almost not got a seat.

Lucy was silent as she looked over the shelves again. He counted the beats before her curiosity won.

'No other family photos?'

Eight. Not bad—he'd been starting to think she'd be able to contain it. Should have known better. Lucy lacked control. He already knew that. 'No other family.'

'What about your mum?'

No stopping her now.

'My mother left my father after fifteen years of marriage. She remarried and has two other children.' Brief summary of fact. She'd cheated. Found herself someone else. Daniel had never been able to understand it. What the hell had the woman wanted? His father was rich, successful, driven to achieve—for her—and she'd thrown it all in his face.

'Did you go with her?'

'No.' He could see her now, standing at the door, calling his name, just the once. He'd shaken his head. He'd been so angry with her for breaking up what he'd thought had been a perfect world. She'd turned and walked away. She hadn't even fought for him.

'How old were you?'

'Fourteen.'

'Your dad's a lawyer?'

'Yes.' He answered in the way he instructed his defendants to—honest but brief. Never offer more than you were asked for.

'He works long hours?'

'Yes.'

Her frown was growing. 'So what did you do after school?'

'After swimming I would go to his office and do my homework in the library.' He was heartily sick of this interrogation and irritated with himself for putting up with it this long. He had the horrible impression pity had just crossed her face. He certainly didn't deserve that. He and his father had established a good life. Both had launched further into work. His dad had hired a housekeeper and given up on women—instructing Daniel never to bother with them, never to trust.

Daniel had worked hard at his studies, hard at his swimming and, when older, hard at playing the field. He'd found a happy balance—of enjoying what women had to offer without risking his heart.

Because nobody, but nobody, was walking out on Daniel again.

His greatest lesson had been self-reliance.

He took the photo, put it on the shelf and turned the questions back on her. 'What about you—your parents split up?' They all seemed to, eventually—in spirit, if not physically.

She looked surprised. 'No, not at all. They have a really happy marriage.' A look of rue crossed her face. 'But they didn't do such a great job of parenting.'

'Marriage and children inevitably end in disaster,' Daniel replied crisply. 'I don't intend ever committing to either.'

Lucy froze, meeting his wintry gaze squarely—and saw the implacable set to his jaw. That was her told, then. He really meant it too. Crazily, she felt sorry for him. Despite what he'd said at the temp agency, Lucy knew they differed. Sure, she didn't commit to long-term work, but that didn't mean she didn't want a long-term relationship, or children even—in the future. A long way in the future. Maybe. Assuming she met someone who'd actually fall for her. Who'd actually believe in her—warts and all.

Her 'feeling sorry for' vibe turned inwards. She shrugged it, and the soft thoughts of him, off. 'I have to get going. Thanks for the room. I'll try to get a place sorted as soon as I can.'

Not waiting for a reply, not wanting to take in just how fine he looked at the moment, she left. Walking briskly towards town, she realised she was starving. She figured she'd head straight for the club and eat there. One take-out Thai curry later, she was temporarily warm on the inside again and kidding herself she'd moved on. Being with Daniel had definitely been a huge mistake and she'd totally done the right thing by breezing over it and putting it behind them. But she couldn't shake him from her mind completely. Instead she slowly digested the info. Ruminated for several hours, in fact. She'd caught a glimpse of one very angry young man. His mother had left his father—and him. And though she knew he'd deny it, he'd been hurt and had frozen over as a result. Well, Lucy didn't have the reserves to warm him through. She had issues of her own to deal with. Past demons that popped up when you least expected them, a permanent feeling of idiocy and inferiority, and the doubt that she'd ever find the place where she'd fit in.

But she still wanted him. Her body wanted more of the ecstasy he'd unleashed. She couldn't look at the pool table without a tide of heat to her face. Grimacing, she reached across the bar and felt muscles stiff from a workout they hadn't had in quite a while. Or ever.

Thankfully the doors opened and she became too busy to dwell on it further. There was no sign of Daniel the entire evening and she was glad, glad, glad.

She got home a little after four. She knew she was too pumped to have any chance of sleep and so, after stripping to her sleeping attire of singlet and panties, headed to the kitchen. She stood in the doorway of the fridge and nearly jumped a foot when she heard the front door opening. Daniel appeared. In full tuxedo. Oh, my. James Bond was nothing on this guy. His jacket sat snug across his broad swimmer's shoulders. Clean lines. The black and white suited him, damn it.

She stared, wondering for a moment if her insomnia-addled brain was playing tricks on her and this was some sort of heavenly hallucination.

'Can't sleep?'

No. He was real.

She shook her head. 'Just getting some warm milk.'

He nodded. 'Put enough in for me, will you? I think I'll be needing it too.' His tone was bland but she risked a quick glance. With the only light in the kitchen coming from the open fridge door, those gold-tinged eyes were giving nothing away. She looked over his tux again. Tried not to be attracted to it but failed.

She reminded herself that people in power—and Daniel was on his way to that—didn't listen. Didn't care. Daniel would be no different. She poured some milk into a jug. Painfully aware of how little she was wearing, she turned her back to him, keeping an eye on the milk in the microwave, compelled to make small talk to slice through her heavy awareness. 'Good night?'

'Yes. How was the club?'

'Good. Busy.'

'Good.'

End of conversation. Beginning of surreptitious looks. She encountered his gaze every time. Her stress level increased, and her body temperature soared as wicked wants started whispering in her mind. Too scary. She flashed back to the moment on the pool table when she'd come to—where after the initial terror she'd relaxed completely in his arms again. Too vulnerable. Thankfully the microwave pinged and she grabbed two mugs and filled them. Snatching one from the counter, she clutched it to her and headed away quickly. Her mind had latched onto the one thing that she knew would be an instant cure for insomnia.

Rampant sex.

'Hope you get some sleep.' His voice was low and a little

husky and he didn't move as she walked away from the kitchen, meaning she had to brush past just that bit too close. She squawked some sort of unintelligible reply and practically ran to her room. The recovery time was a good two hours.

Nights passed as Lucy worked in the bar. She worked hard and slept little. Tiredness made every bone creak but she refused to acknowledge it—she was determined to work harder than ever. She'd show Daniel exactly how good she was at this job—that she was mediocre no more. For once in her life she was going to shine.

The staff told her the bar was busier than usual. She'd love to think it had something to do with her, but probably it was a result of the incredibly warm weather they were having this week. The idea that she was influencing the success of the bar would be too good to be true.

Yet Isabel suggested otherwise. 'Lara just liked having a place to hang with her mates. It was never a serious business venture for her. She never bothered with that side of it; she left it to the manager and he was useless.'

Lucy had figured that—given the state of the office. The club had only been open a year and the paperwork was in a mess. She rolled up her sleeves and discovered putting things in order was actually enjoyable. She must have inherited more of her father's accountancy gene than she'd realised. She worked late night after night and hid in her room until she was sure Daniel had gone to work for the day. Really she should be moving out, but until she saw the first pay cheque she had little option but to stay where she was.

She didn't see him again until after one of her shifts later that week. This time he was the one raiding the fridge and not wearing enough clothing.

'Warm milk?' The thread of humour was so thin she wondered if she'd dreamt it.

She shook her head. Unable to speak at the sight of him in

his boxers. For a few days there she'd thought she'd got over him. It only took one second of seeing him again to return her pulse to agitated state and her desire to fever pitch. The worst thing was he knew—he saw the flame in her face before she established the control to cover it. His eyes narrowed. They engaged in one of their silent staring duels—and she was first to look away.

The following night she let Isabel and Corey finish up, getting herself to the apartment by eleven p.m. Vainly hoping for a decent sleep. Impossible. She listened for signs of Daniel—none. By midnight he still hadn't walked in the door. He worked way too hard. She felt irrationally irritable and there was only one cure for that. She rifled through her CD file and, with favourite in hand, marched to his state-of-the-art stereo system. She put in the disc and pressed the button. The music blared. She smiled. Dancing was her answer to everything—freedom on her terms. Alone, wild and crazy—giving up control, just letting her mind go and her body move to the music. Safe. She didn't go dancing to pick up a guy, she went to be free. To have fun. And that was why she found herself loving this job, because she could create the environment for others to do the same.

But in Daniel's apartment right now she felt restricted—by her attraction to him, and the feeling of vulnerability that came with it. She was stunned she'd slept in his arms. It scared her. What scared her more was the feeling of safety she'd had in them. But her instinct had been well wrong on that count. He'd backed off faster than a hirsute man offered a chest wax.

She pushed the worry from her mind, turned up the volume and focused on the beat. Dance crazy and she'd wear herself out so she could sleep—that was the aim, and nothing beat dancing wildly to her favourite group. Stomping her feet and slapping her thighs, she was having a fine old time working out pure frustration.

Then the music suddenly stopped. She whirled around and

saw Daniel standing at the stereo. He was impeccably dressed as ever except for the curious expression on his face. At least he wasn't flat on the floor laughing.

'You always do what you want, when you want to?'

She cleared her throat nervously. 'No.' If she did she'd be over there and on him about now. If he didn't look so disapproving.

'Music's a little loud for my neighbours downstairs. It's late.'

She snatched back her mettle. 'Wouldn't want them thinking you were having fun, Daniel.'

'It's not possible to have fun to country music, Lucy.'

'You think? You should try it some time.' She cast a disparaging look over him, flicked her hair with an air of studied nonchalance and hoped she could saunter to her bedroom.

'What's with this attitude towards honest, hard-working men in suits? Don't you like the work ethic it represents?'

'It doesn't represent work ethic. It represents power, authority, status.'

'What's wrong with that?'

'I have an aversion to authority.' He stood for everything she couldn't stand—arrogance and an inability to understand.

'Really.' He laughed. 'Do tell.'

'I prefer an individual approach to life. I don't like being told what to do—by anyone.'

'So you're the arty, flaky type through and through.'

She stopped her bad saunter and glared at him.

He strolled towards her. 'You think you're so cool, don't you? No boring office wear for you in your funky, feathery clothes.' He gestured to her multi-layered look. 'You couldn't possibly be so dull as to hold down a nine-to-five kind of job, couldn't bear to be in an office, behind a desk. Take on responsibility. How awful that would be.' He moved a little closer. His voice lowered to a whisper. 'Well, let me tell you something, Trouble. There is nothing remotely cool about country music.'

Lucy stared at him. 'You're so wrong.' *About everything.* She stepped a little closer to deliver her parting shot. 'I am cool, cool like funky. But you know what? You're cool too—cool like *frozen.*'

A great white shark had nothing on his smile. 'You think?'

'Yeah, you're so "in control".'

Daniel watched her hightail it to her room. In control? Hardly. He was on a knife-edge. Dangerously close to acting on emotional impulse and grabbing her to him and kissing her senseless—until the biting backchat was replaced by the soft sighs and the screams of satisfaction he'd wrung from her last week.

She was the one who was wrong. *About everything.*

He prowled through his lounge feeling like an intruder. Her shoes were parked at the end of the sofa. Her sarong was draped across the cushions at the end. A magazine lay upside down in the middle of the floor. He picked it up to put it on the coffee-table. His eyebrow rose at one of the headlines on the cover—TEN WAYS TO DRIVE HIM WILD. She didn't need the magazine. She could write the authoritative book on that in ten minutes. He sat on the sofa and flung the magazine out of sight. Stared straight ahead for a minute, but the bright sarong leapt out at the corner of his eye. He sighed, gave in, and picked it up. It was vividly coloured but soft to touch. Just like her. Beautiful, outrageous but with a hint of vulnerability—the chink he had yet to figure out but knew was there.

He'd honestly thought being with her once would be enough. He was dedicated to his work and ordinarily he refused the distraction of a monogamous series of dates, let alone an actual relationship. He'd never be humiliated the way his mother had humiliated his father. He wasn't ever going to be left for anyone or anything. And his drive to succeed was for his own satisfaction—no one else's.

But he wanted Lucy again and knew she still wanted him. It was apparent every time their paths crossed. Maybe he should take time out to ensure their paths crossed frequently. She was only going to be around a fortnight or so anyway. He wanted another experience with that hot, wild woman he'd discovered on the pool table.

Wanted, not needed. Just once more.

CHAPTER EIGHT

You enjoy an active and fast-paced environment

THAT night Lucy worked even later than usual, spending the whole time trying to ignore the memories of the previous Friday. She was trying to stop wishing it would all happen again. Regretting the way she'd nailed the lid on it so soon despite knowing it had well been for the best. He annoyed the pants off her—literally. But the last thing she needed was to get involved with a guy—hot as he was—who could offer as much emotional support as a stuffed frog. If she was going to open up to someone, he needed to be nice, and capable of showing some kind of understanding—not clashing with her at every opportunity and being Mr Bossy.

She got home at just after six in the morning—when the first joggers were already out pounding along by the waterfront. She'd attempted a grin at one woman speeding by but it was more of a grimace. She stood under the shower for a few heavenly moments before slipping straight into bed, pulling just the cotton sheet over her naked, warm, slightly wet body.

What felt like five minutes later there was a knock on her door. Groggily she opened one eye. 'What?'

'Lucy.'

'Go away.'

He didn't. Rather he opened the door. Tee shirt and long shorts. Tanned muscles on show. She shut her eyes tight. The last thing she needed was to see Daniel looking gorgeous in casual-wear. *Self-control, self-control*—she had some, didn't she? Even a teeny bit?

He yanked open her curtains. She screwed her eyes shut tighter against the glare.

'Lucy, you're coming out with me.'

'No. I'm sleeping.' With him. In her dreams. All the time.

'Open your eyes.'

She ignored him.

'When did you last see the sun?' She could feel him close by the bed. 'You're turning into some vampire. The bar is going great, but you're working all hours. You look awful. I'm ordering you to take the night off.'

She opened her eyes at that. 'Are you forbidding me to go there?'

He nodded. 'If you set foot in that bar in the next twenty-four hours I'm sacking you.'

'You can't do that.'

'I'm the boss.'

She closed her eyes again. 'Fine. I won't go. Now leave me alone.'

'No. I'll stand here and annoy you until you get out of bed and spend the day in fresh air like normal people.'

'Daniel.'

'Would you rather I got in there with you?'

She sat up immediately, clutching the sheet to her chest.

He grinned. 'Thought that idea might get you moving.' He strolled to her door. 'I'll give you five minutes. If you're not dressed and in the lounge by then I'll be back in here and dressing you myself.'

She lay down again after he left and debated whether or not to stay there.

No. She pushed back the covers and looked out from the

curtains, amazed to see the sun high in the sky. She quickly slipped on a top. Then she heard his voice. 'Put your swimsuit on.'

That would be the bikini—the only swimsuit she had. She really must go shopping for an all-covering granny special soon. She pulled the top off and put the bikini on underneath. Her heart's tempo picked up. She shouldn't. Shouldn't, shouldn't.

Lucy had always struggled with *shouldn't.* It was the red rag and she was the bull.

They walked along the bay and found a warm spot on the crowded beach. He had a blanket.

'Your tan is fading.' He ran light fingers down her arm. She shut her eyes with the agony of it and hoped he couldn't see her reaction flare behind her Jackie O sunglasses.

'Why are we here, Daniel?'

'My case starts next week. This is my last chance to relax for a while. And you need a break.'

'What's your case about?'

He stared into the sea. 'The last thing I want to think about right now is that case.'

'What do you want to think about?'

'Nothing. No thoughts. No analysis.'

No regrets. He blinked and turned to look at her.

'Let's go for that swim.' She raised her brow, wanting to shatter the sudden stillness. 'Race you to the pontoon.' She'd ripped off her glasses and dress and was running to the water before she'd finished the sentence. She heard his growl of laughter, and knew her head start would only be a split-second advantage.

The water was freezing but she struck out and pulled her arms through the water furiously. Ten seconds into it and she was fighting a stitch-like pain in her side. How could she have lost fitness in just a few days? Breathless, she finally got there and tried really hard not to be completely peeved as she saw his face already bobbing by the wood.

'Your technique's not bad really,' he said. 'You could do with a bit of practice.'

'You think?' She puffed out the words.

A party of keen teenagers splashed out, swamping the pontoon with wet bodies. Lucy sank a little in the crowd. Daniel frowned as he saw her face. He reached out an arm and pulled her to him. He gripped the pontoon and supported her with his other arm. 'You OK?'

'Sure.' Her breath wouldn't return. If anything she felt more puffed. And cold. She wanted his other arm around her. His legs brushed against hers as he trod the water.

'Your lips are blue. You're freezing.'

All she could think about was how he could warm her up.

'I'll swim you back in.'

This was embarrassing. It was only a few metres but her body was acting as if she'd tried to swim the English channel in winter with only a banana for breakfast. Come to think of it, she hadn't had breakfast. Or lunch.

'OK.'

'Put your arms and legs around me.'

'Sorry?'

'Come on, koala hold.'

'You can't swim with me like that.'

'I can swim. Trust me.' He took her hands and pulled her towards him. She had no option, had to cling to him like a little barnacle on a big rock. Oh, yeah, she just had to.

His body was warm even in the chilly water. The feeling of security in his strong arms was soporific, the pleasure in being carried by a fit male extreme.

I am pathetic. I am a pathetic excuse for a modern woman. I should be swimming myself. She relaxed against him completely and let her arms hold him close. The sensation was too nice not to indulge. Her eyes shut tight. Her body wasn't cold any more.

'Lucy, you can let go now.'

She opened her eyes to his dry amusement, suddenly aware she was barely under the water. A boy who looked about eight years old was standing in the water not far away. She really was pathetic. Reluctantly she looked up into his face. He stared at her, his mouth sort of smiling, but his eyes were like arrows piercing deep, searching. Talk about one-way traffic—hunting out her thoughts while refusing to reveal any of his own. She dropped her gaze, landing on his shoulders instead. Stupid, because they were very broad and she was very nearly *clinging*. She went to lower her legs but his hands tightened on her a fraction. She risked another look at his eyes. Gleaming gold flecks grew—bringing warmth to his usually reserved demeanour—and bringing heat to her belly.

The young boy hollered out to a friend. The moment shattered. She slipped from his arms and stumbled up the beach. Back on shore she shivered. Need made her bones ache. He handed her a towel and she sat with it cloaked tepee-style around her. She caught his frown.

'I'm OK, just tired.'

'You haven't eaten.' He rummaged in his bag and pulled out a banana. She giggled.

'What's so funny?' He peeled the banana. 'OK, it's not much. Down that and we'll go to the deli.'

They sat and waited for their order. He picked up a paper from the counter. He took the news section, offered her the glossy magazine.

'Actually I'd prefer the world section.'

He looked curious.

'Weirdest-stories-in-the-world section,' she explained. 'You know—SHARK EATS ELEPHANT, EIGHTY-NINE-YEAR-OLD WOMAN GIVES BIRTH.'

'That's not the world section, that's tabloid.' He handed it to her anyway. 'I'll have it back when you're done.'

The silence was almost companionable. He sat in his long

board shorts, sandals and nothing else. She wore a tee and her sarong tied round her middle. If she closed her eyes she could pretend they were on a beach on some remote Pacific island. Only they wouldn't have a table separating them. She wouldn't be avoiding eye contact. There wouldn't be other people sitting too close and talking too loudly about what movie they should go to that night. He wouldn't be so engrossed in the business section.

The pancakes with banana, bacon and maple syrup looked fantastic, but only a few bites into it she abandoned it—grumpily recognising her appetite was nothing like normal.

They wandered the few yards back to his flat. She'd pretended the silence was comfortable, but now it intensified to uneasy awareness. They said nothing as they climbed the stairs. Once in the apartment she headed straight to her room, showered and re-dressed. She headed to the lounge and out to the balcony. She sat and took in the view and pretended she couldn't care less where he was right now or what he was doing.

He wasn't interested. Nor was she.

She was a big fat liar.

She turned to see what he was doing. He stood at the table—currently scattered with paperwork from one end to the other. He must have showered because his hair was freshly damp. She tried not to think about his body naked under the jets but the sight of him in those jeans didn't take the edge off. To her dismay he started loading the papers into a box.

'You're not staying in tonight?' Why had she thought he would? Just because he'd made her take the night off—he hadn't suggested a date or anything like it.

'I have to work.' He shuffled more paper. 'I worked all morning and now I've had a break I need to get back into it. The case starts soon.'

'You can't work here?' He'd worked here this morning, hadn't he?

His hands stilled. 'No. I can't.' His lips twisted. 'I need to meet with my junior and go for as long as it takes.' He clipped the lid on the box. 'You stay home and watch a movie or something. I spoke to Sinead and she's promised to have everything under control.'

'I should go there tonight.'

'You've been working too many long hours. I'm not risking your taking me to the Employment Tribunal for unreasonable working conditions. You need a day off.' He walked out, shut the door and took her good mood with him.

She sat for a while, thought about food and decided against it. She headed indoors, switched on the TV and flicked through the channels—once through all of them, then again before switching it off. She checked out the bookcases again. Other than legal mumbo jumbo there was only a selection of modern classics, a few wine almanacs and a collection of crime novels. Typical. The last thing she liked to read. Where was the light relief?

She couldn't stand it any more. She was so out of place here, with nothing in common for them. It screamed of Daniel. And all she wanted was Daniel. Being in his space like this was driving her insane.

She grabbed her light jacket, set of keys and headed for the door.

She stopped at the Malaysian restaurant near the pool and got a curry to take away. The spicy aroma tempted her listless appetite and she headed to the club with a spring in her step.

Sinead rolled her eyes as Lucy approached her on the door. 'You're supposed to be having a night off.'

'I am. I'm going to sneak this into the back, then I'm going to have a game of pool and relax.'

'Yeah, right, you'll be back behind that bar before you can help yourself.'

Sinead was right. But, Lucy mentally argued, it was a particularly busy night. A film crew had wrapped and the club was the post-party destination point. The place heaved with beautiful people all wanting drinks right this instant. Corey and the other tenders pounced on Lucy as soon as they saw her. Lucy loved it. It felt great to be wanted. Fantastic to be needed.

She slugged back her food and, after a freshen-up, headed out to face the punters.

It was after eleven when she spotted Daniel. Her heart stopped, then accelerated alarmingly. He'd just entered with a couple of guys at his side. Lawyers-doing-casual. But it wasn't them who caught her attention. It was the striking-looking brunette on the other side of him. She was tall—almost as tall as Sinead. Slim with perfectly formed corkscrew curls ringletting around her face. It made Lucy loathe her own unruly waves. The brunette wore a black top—close-fitting, showing off her small waist and gentle rounded curves. She'd teamed it with a royal-blue skirt—slim line with a pencil-pleated trim around the bottom. Underneath her long shapely legs tapered to slender ankles and stylish shoes. Definitely a lawyer. Definitely interested in Daniel. It was obvious in one second—the way she looked at him, the way she stood close to him.

Question—was Daniel interested in her?

Lucy looked to his face—although usually it was inscrutable. Only when she was up close and able to see the changing molten gold in his eyes did she have some idea of what he was thinking—and feeling.

But right now he wasn't wearing his usual poker expression. He was looking straight at her, and he was looking mad. She glanced again at the woman by his side, the one standing too close. He'd told Lucy not to come here tonight. Was this why? He didn't want his one-night stand getting anywhere near his *girlfriend?* Is that who she was—his girlfriend?

Damn lying lawyer.

Lucy squared her shoulders and turned to the next customer waiting. Hiding her rising fury with über-efficiency.

Within minutes Daniel was standing at his usual spot on the end of her bar, alone. 'Lucy.'

She finished serving the customer she was dealing with and turned to the next.

'Lucy.' Her hair stood on end. That wasn't a tone she'd heard from him before.

She smiled an apology to the customer after that and turned towards Daniel. He glared at her grimly, grabbed her arm and pulled her close so he could talk right into her face. 'What are you doing here?'

She glared right back. 'What does it look like?'

'I told you not to come in here tonight.'

She tried not to be dazzled by the molten gold. 'I'm a free agent.'

'I told you I'd sack you.'

'Go right ahead. You can serve all these people yourself.' Any sense of camaraderie they'd shared that afternoon was smashed.

He glanced along the bar—people queuing four or five deep the length of it. He glowered. 'You can work out your notice period—tonight.'

Hell. He really was mad.

'Fine.'

She turned her back on him and stomped back a few paces to serve another customer. Lying, cheating jerk. How on earth could she still want this guy? How was it possible she wanted him more than ever right this very instant? She wanted to pounce on him, knock him back on the table and show him exactly who was boss. Wanted to fight it out in the most passionate way.

And he'd win, of course. Then he'd be able to walk away and she'd be left wanting more.

That knowledge made her even madder. She glanced back to him and met his angry stare full on. For the next ten minutes he stood at the end of the bar and they traded optical daggers.

When she looked up at the next customer she stiffened to see it was the brunette blessed with legs that went for ever. Her big brown eyes weren't exactly warm and friendly.

'You know Daniel?' Straight to the point.

Lucy smiled—saccharine. 'Sure.'

'I'm Sarah. I work with him. And you are?'

'Lucy.' So Sarah wasn't a girlfriend—yet. But if the proprietary air was anything to go by, it wouldn't be long.

'You're a friend?'

This woman was definitely a lawyer—the way she shot out questions. Irritated, Lucy decided to toss in a spanner. 'Actually we live together.'

She saw the other woman's eyes widen. If it didn't matter so much she'd have laughed at the look on her face. 'Really? I didn't know Daniel was seriously involved with anyone. Rumour is he's a two-dates-and-it's-over player.'

Lucy poured the drinks and tried to hide the shake in her hand. 'He likes to keep his personal life personal. Sorry.'

Her adversary went to pay.

'On the house.' It wasn't a needle of guilt Lucy felt, more like a chainsaw. What was she doing interfering in Daniel's life? This woman might turn out to be the love of his life—she certainly fitted the 'polished' bill. But if that was the case, what was he doing having sex with Lucy in the middle of the night? Especially mind-blowing, best-in-all-your-life sex. Unless it hadn't been for him. Maybe that was just normal. Oh, God. She had to stop this agonising. She felt the itch in the soles of her feet; she should cut and run. But then she looked about the bar, saw the happy crowds and wanted to stay. And she saw the tall, dark, unfairly handsome suit striding back to his lawyer mates and really, really didn't want to leave.

Daniel was seriously annoyed. The woman was tired. She'd been working far too hard all week—not a day off, crazy long hours, and she was growing paler by the minute. And he couldn't stop thinking about her. He had a complex case starting and here he was worrying about some woman he'd known less than a fortnight. She was contrary. She was ornery. She was everything he didn't need.

And she was so beautiful.

He couldn't keep his eyes off her. She distracted him. He'd had to get out of the flat after this afternoon. He'd worked well enough in the morning but the knowledge she was sleeping in the next room had called to him. Until he'd been able to stand it no longer and he'd got her up. Wanting to spend time with her. Wanting to know if she wanted more. He suspected, but he wanted certainty.

He'd been playing it cool all week but he was dangerously close to flaring. He'd worked in the office tonight with the team because he'd needed to escape her presence in his apartment. Perversely he'd come to the club after to relax, because he felt oddly at home on his barstool. But he didn't want *her* to be here. He just wanted to be in her space without having her there stretching his nerves to break point. He was fast losing the fight against the out-of-control desire to have her again.

Sarah appeared in front of him and handed him a whiskey. His thoughts were halted with her direct comment.

'You're a dark horse.'

She smiled but he could see sharpness in her eyes. Something had set his junior on edge.

'Why's that?'

'I didn't know you were living with someone.'

He looked to where she looked.

Lucy.

The gulp of whiskey burned. 'She told you?'

As they watched her pulling a pint Lucy looked over to them. Her quickly hidden startle pleased him. She turned away as soon as she saw his gaze on her. Out of the corner of his eye he kept watching her and within an instant she was looking their way again. And away. And back. Much as she wanted to she couldn't help herself. He knew the feeling.

He savoured the whiskey this time and the fire inside had nothing to do with the swallow. His smile was big and wide. 'Yeah. She's something, isn't she?'

'She's…not what I'd have expected.'

'No.' He grinned again.

'It's serious between you?'

Daniel stared at the content of his glass and made an ambiguous 'mmm' response. Of course it wasn't. But he had to quell the crazy urge to punch a fist in the air. His drifter bar manager was jealous. You could only be jealous when you cared.

So there was his certainty. Proof positive. Meaning her reluctance was surmountable. He wanted the next few hours to fast forward. He wanted to be back in his apartment—just him and her. It was definitely time to sort a few things out. Such as who was on top.

He took another sip of whiskey. She didn't know it but Lucy had done him another favour. Now as far as Sarah was concerned he was well off the market. Excellent. Sarah had 'interested' and 'power couple' written all over her. Hell would freeze over first. While Sarah would know of his love-and-leave reputation, Daniel also knew she was as tenacious as a dog with a bone. He'd been careful not to give her even the slightest encouragement and now this should seal it completely.

Feeling happier than he had all week, he hid his smile from Lucy as she scowled at him. He was going to enjoy turning her into that sighing, sexy creature again. Meantime he could afford to turn the screws on her a little. She had a jealous wound? Time for a little salt. He sent Sarah and the boys out ahead of him. Then he approached her.

It took every ounce of self-control not to reach out and haul her to him. He badly wanted to kiss her into submission. He wanted to see her body arch up to him, see her eyelids flutter, hear her moan of delight.

Soon.

'Keep up the good work.' He said it as patronisingly as he could—loving the fact that he'd be on the floor like a dead ant if her look had its way. 'I'm taking Sarah home.' He turned and winked. 'Don't wait up.'

CHAPTER NINE

You have good control over your desires and temptations

LUCY stomped about in the kitchen, banging cupboard doors and returning plates home from the dishwasher with more force than necessary. The night had dragged after Daniel had left. Bitter, she muttered nasty things under her breath. It was ridiculous given that she was the one who'd said no. And she'd been right to say no. She'd asked for everything he had to offer and promised him the same. The trouble was she had a lot more to give than him—a heart, for starters.

No sign he was home yet, so the nasty murmurings increased in audibility. He'd be cosied up to Sarah about now. Lucy would move out tomorrow. Even the dreaded hostel would be better than staying here. She'd go pack her bag now. That would make her feel better.

She turned to do just that and got the fright of her life to find Daniel standing right behind her.

'Everything OK?'

Of course not. He was in boxers and nothing but. Not what she needed. Why didn't he wear full-length pyjamas and a hideous dressing gown? She lashed out. 'What are you doing here?'

'It's my home. I was trying to sleep but that's impossible with the racket you're making.' He took a step nearer. 'Something the matter?'

'No,' she snapped, grabbing a glass from the shelf.

'Why did you tell Sarah we're living together?'

He shocked her with his directness. Uncomfortable heat rose in her cheeks. She tried to shrug it off. 'We are living together.'

'Under the same roof, sure, but that wasn't the innocent impression Sarah got and I'm sure you didn't mean it that innocently.'

She filled the glass with water. 'I'm sorry if I made things difficult for you.'

'No, you're not.' Pause. 'For the record, I'm not and never have been interested in Sarah.'

'Oh.' She turned, her back right against the bench. He'd stepped even nearer. 'She's not your type?'

'No.'

She feigned extreme interest in the glass of water. 'You must be awfully hard to please.'

'Oh, I don't know. You did OK the other night.'

Smash. The glass hit the floor. She bent to it instantly. Heart thudding, she grabbed at the shards. 'I'm as bad as Corey.' Glass pierced as she tried to gather the bits—futile, seeing there was no way it could be glued back together. Her anger dissolved. Melancholy remained.

'Stop. It's only a glass. It doesn't matter.' He seized her wrist. 'Don't move. I don't want you to cut your foot as well.'

Obediently she stayed still while he got a brush and dustpan and swept away the fragments, and she couldn't help admiring his muscular legs and strong forearms. He wrapped the glass in paper and discarded it.

She stayed on the ground, hoping he'd leave before she threw herself at him.

He didn't. 'Let me see your hand.' He crouched beside her so he could see her properly. 'Lucy.'

She held out her hand. He took it and gently uncurled her fingers. A fine line of red crossed her palm.

'I'll get a plaster.' He soft-footed out to the bathroom and was back in a few minutes. She hadn't moved.

'So stupid. I don't know what's the matter with me.' She sniffed—most unladylike. 'I'm not sleeping too well.' It was the story of her life. 'I can't sleep.'

He finished smoothing the plaster, then looked at her. 'Neither can I.'

She met his eyes with hers. Her hand shook in his and he closed his fingers around it. Keeping it steady with a warm, firm grip.

He stood and made her stand with him. 'Maybe we could help each other out?'

His lips were so close and he tilted her chin with a finger to bring hers nearer. Her lids fluttered lower so she wouldn't have to look into his eyes and openly admit defeat.

The finger under her chin pulled her another inch closer and with a small sigh she melted. There was no hesitation—she was unable to resist a second longer. She opened for him, reached for him, curling her fingers into the hair at the back of his head. Sweet relief flooded through her as his arms went around her and hauled her close—he wanted her. He held back from the kiss. She could feel him studying her. She refused to open her eyes but leaned against him, wordlessly wanting him to understand she was so very willing.

She heard him half laugh under his breath, then felt him slip his arm under her knees to scoop her up. He made her feel weightless, wanted. He strode quickly, surely. She kept her eyes shut and let her body simply feel. The strength of his arms as they held her—as close as they'd been in the water, but this was better because she knew she was about to get it all from him. She could hardly wait.

She felt the mattress beneath her and was sorry when his arms slipped from under her. But satisfaction soon followed as she felt the bed depress with his weight, heard the foil rip and knew he was ready. Then his hands were on her, stroking the skin her top exposed. He pulled up the hem so her stomach was bared. His fingers traced the path, his lips followed. She shook as they touched her, her muscles spasmed involuntarily. He responded immediately, his hands sliding to where her breasts were bursting from her bra. Hard, overly sensitive nipples that ached for his hot mouth. She moaned as he read her mind and closed over her, sucking her nipple in—material and all. Her legs parted immediately as he pressed his weight onto her lower body. He unbuttoned her top with quick fingers and simply pushed the cups of her bra down so her breasts spilled over. He took them in his hands and tasted. Teased. She arched back, baring her neck, straining her pelvis up.

There were too many clothes—despite his near nudity. Again he read her mind. He rolled, quickly removing her skirt. No slow unwrapping this time. Her panties flew through the air. Then her bra. Then his boxers. He leant over her again and they were almost together in one mad moment. He held back—just—and instead teased her, his hand in place between her legs as his mouth devoured hers. He lifted his head a little as his fingers played harder. With amusement in his eye he watched her reaction.

She sucked in a gasp of air and for a second the fog of lust cleared. This was not a good idea. She'd get emotional. He wouldn't. But she closed her eyes, closing her brain down—refusing to let it ruin such a good time.

He wasn't having it. 'Open your eyes, Lucy,' he muttered as he nibbled on her neck.

She screwed them tighter.

'Open them or I stop.'

She opened them.

'Got anything to say?'

'Like what?'

'Please.'

She clamped her mouth shut.

He grinned. 'I'm really going to enjoy making you say it.'

Oh, she hoped so. Naughty Lucy.

'Because that's what you really want, isn't it? Me to do my best to make you.' He laughed.

Damn. He could read her like a book.

So she flipped it open. 'Oh, Daniel. Make love to me.' It was her best Marilyn Monroe impersonation ever—laced with a slurp of irony.

'You're going to have to do better than that, Trouble. I want genuine. Desperate. *Need.*'

He bent to attend to her breasts again and she gave his ceiling a rueful smile. She was seconds away from admitting all that and more. He began to work his way down her body—kissing, caressing, turning up the heat. It was magic how he became so hot and made her feel as if he were worshipping her body. He made her feel so wanted—every cell in her was on fire. He'd gone straight to the furnace and was stoking it, fuelling her until she was hotter than she'd ever been. Driving her relentlessly close, so close, to climax.

He touched her again, deep into her core. 'The other night you said you didn't want this again.'

'I…' *can't speak*—not when he was toying with her like that.

His thumb rubbed her. 'You weren't that attracted.'

She lifted her hips up, pushing against him. Wanting this but more than this. Wanting the whole lot of him.

He rubbed that little bit harder and faster. His fingers delved deeper. 'Will you admit that was wrong?'

He kissed her belly. Heat—desire-fuelled and that of pure irritation—flooded her. 'Is this how you cross-examine your witnesses?' She moaned. 'No wonder you always win.'

She felt his smile on her stomach. He continued his tortuous path downwards. 'Part of my job involves assessing whether people are telling the truth or not.' His mouth reached the point where his thumb still worked. 'I'm pretty good at my job.'

His mouth replaced the thumb—his tongue flicking, while his fingers, still deep, moved faster.

She cried out, raking his shoulders with her hands.

'What?' he asked, his hot breath nearly destroying her.

'Please, please, please.'

He moved quickly, his fingers gone, his humour vanished. In a split second he was on top of her, his body holding hers down. She could feel his erection right against her. So, so close—she nearly cried with the need of it.

He took her hands in his and lifted them so they were pinned by her ears. Right at the point of entry he stopped, fixing her with his gaze, cold gold sparks penetrating. She stared up at him. Stilled by the intensity and ferocity in his face.

His grip tightened on her almost to the point of pain. He spoke, passion audible. '*Never* lie to me again.'

She gasped. She wanted him so much, but was terrified of how far he saw—right through her. Every last inch. She blinked rapidly. 'OK.'

He surged forward—knowing her inside and out. She gasped again, a silent scream as she got the one thing she'd been wanting all week. It was better than she remembered. Better than she'd dreamed.

His grip on her hands loosened and she adjusted hers—lacing her fingers through his. Locking them in that position—just as their bodies were now locked: eye to eye, palm to palm, thigh to thigh. One.

Their gaze remained unbroken. She saw his anger and lust. She'd never been so close to anyone, never seen naked desire like this. Never felt such frustration and basic emotion on show. She knew her face reflected the same.

Their bodies embraced, closer, ever closer. So intense was her consciousness that she came close to circuiting out, but she couldn't bear to close her eyes. Impossible—she couldn't break away from him. Lines had been opened between them, like a channel to the soul. She found it as fascinating as she did terrifying.

She'd never had sex like this.

She'd never made love like this.

As his hips pressed to meet her rising ones, as he worked deeper and deeper in, the intensity grew. The more she wanted to look away, the more she couldn't. And then her body shorted and took the decision away from her. As the ecstasy hit her eyelids fluttered and his face was lost to her for moments as her body shook and his name passed unthinkingly, unwillingly from her lips again and again.

When she opened her eyes again it was to find his still bearing down on her, watching her surrender to the joy he'd given her with pure satisfaction. She wanted the same for him. She wanted him to have the same pleasure in her arms that she got from his. Her fingers flexed. He must have seen the desire in her eyes because his mouth twisted into a smile. He bent his head and kissed her, his mouth possessing as deeply and fully as the rest of his body already was—and she kissed him back with all the honesty she could. Uncaring of the degree to which she was revealing her need for him. He knew it anyway and he didn't like her hiding it. So she gave it free rein. Caressing him, whispering what she wanted, what she liked, asking the same from him, wanting to please him, wanting to make his studious control evaporate. It didn't take that long. His body went rigid and she tasted his groan as it was forced from him. She slipped her fingers from his and wrapped her arms around him, holding him as he came. Embracing all he had—all he was. And, in doing so, came all over again herself.

For long moments after she lay, still trembling, still in shock. She was too scared to look at him so she burrowed under his hot body. She didn't know what to say. She'd just had the most intimate moment of her life and she was terrified.

Eventually he spoke. 'I don't know about you, but I'm still not tired.'

'No.' Right now she didn't think she'd ever sleep again.

Adrenalin raced through her. How had this guy suddenly become everything?

'Still got more energy to burn?' How could he sound so casual after the intensity of that sex? Probably because that was all it was for him—sex.

'Let's burn.' Well, that was all it would be for her too. Sex—she needed it hard, fast and mindless. She needed pure body—not the merging of everything, the total sharing of minutes before. She needed to think of him purely as a source of pleasure—but as she cried out in his arms again, as she felt his body buckle in bliss, she knew she couldn't ever think of him as such an object.

She was in big, big trouble. But as she lay cocooned in his arms his deep, regular breathing soothed her. The cotton sheet cooled her hot, over-sensitive skin and she slept at peace.

She woke in panic. She'd just slept with him. For hours, not minutes. And it felt fantastic. She'd entered a sweet dreamless state. That it had happened freaked her out almost as much as the nightmare that had haunted her for years. How was it she felt so safe with Daniel? When he challenged her every which way? When he was so remote and reserved?

'Are we going to do this again?'

She looked at him. 'Um.'

He stared straight at her, speaking as matter-of-fact as usual. Cut and dried. He could have been discussing a purchase of bread and milk, he sounded so everyday. 'Because frankly I'm keen, but I can't be bothered with the "Oh, no, I don't want to" rubbish I had from you last week.'

Her jaw fell open. He shut it for her with a push of his finger against her chin and gave her a grin that only just let him get away with it.

'I want you. We're good in bed together, Lucy. We might not have much else in common, but we can do satisfaction. And then we both sleep. Noticed that?'

Of course. It was crazy. She felt more rested than she had in years—even though they'd slept only a few hours. But a perfect, deep sleep—the sort she usually dreamed of as she lay awake hour after hour through the dark night. No nightmares. She'd felt secure, safe.

'You're the best cure for insomnia I've ever had.'

'I'm not quite sure that's a compliment.'

He laughed. *'Touché.'* He sat up in the bed, resting his elbows on his raised knees. 'You physically and mentally exhaust me.'

'And that's a good thing?'

'It is, because then I can sleep and that feels fantastic.' He turned and caught her gaze full on again. 'Tell me it isn't the same for you.'

She'd promised him she wouldn't lie. It was the same. Sparring with him, wondering what angle he was coming from. Trying to figure out what the hell was going on in that overly complex brain of his—and trying to hide what was going on in hers—wore her out. And then there was the sex—consuming every ounce of physical energy she had. Leaving her drained yet replete. Exhausted but invigorated. And able to sleep—in his arms.

'I sleep OK with you.' She'd said she wouldn't lie; as far as she was concerned understating things was still allowed.

'So it's a deal, then? We sleep together—all senses of the word.'

She supposed she should say no. Most other women would. Ha—that was a lie: most women would leap at the chance to be with Daniel night after night. His lover credentials were unbeatable. Physique plus technique equals *magnifique.*

She just had to remember there was nothing else on offer here. Merely a deal to sleep with someone—two insomniacs having regular sex in the quest for a decent night's rest after.

Anyway, she shouldn't want anything else, should she? Not from a shining example of modern conservative establishment like Daniel.

'OK.' She nodded. 'Someone to sleep with.' That was all he would be. Her bedmate.

He kissed her. 'I have to go to work. Be here tonight.'

Who was she kidding? When he kissed her like that fantasies of night after night leading to for ever skipped through her head. She frowned. 'After the club?'

He nodded. 'My bed.'

She looked down. She was afraid that, now he'd seen into her once, he'd see all there was to see all the time. That she was turning all female and falling for him. What had happened to her bluffing skills?

He took her chin again and tilted her face back to him. 'No regrets.'

Once more he kissed her—thoroughly, deeply, teasingly. And it was so unfair because now she was left in bed warm and wet and wanting all over once more and he was gone for the day. She should be gone for good. Instead she rolled over and snuggled in the scent of him, in his sheets. So she couldn't say no, but that didn't mean she couldn't come up with a strategy. She'd challenge him right back.

CHAPTER TEN

You find it difficult to switch off from your job

WHEN Lucy got home in the early hours Daniel was lying on the sofa reading, waiting.

'Have you eaten?'

She shook her head and glanced at the spotless kitchen. 'Nor have you.'

'Let's get pizza.' Instead of reaching for the phone, he reached for her instead. He tipped her head back and she opened her mouth and welcomed him with her tongue, her arms, the press of her pelvis against his.

He lifted away fractionally. 'What do you want? Really want. And I don't mean on your pizza.'

'I want to come. I want you to make me come. I want you to come with me.' She'd turned into a nymphomaniac just like that. She'd always craved freedom—rebelled against her family, her school, any form of authority. It was why she loved dancing. But that freedom was nothing on the freedom she'd found in his arms. The way she could be held but made to feel as if she were flying. It was a freedom that kept her chained to him. She needed to combat it—by seeing how far she could push *him.* 'You phone the pizza. I'll be back in a minute.'

His gaze hit on her cowboy hat the minute she came back into the room twirling it. His smile grew. 'You want me to dress up as a cowboy?'

'Oh, no. You've got it all wrong.' She donned the hat at a rakish angle and pouted. 'I'm the one who does the riding.'

He put on an appalling western accent. 'Well, jump on, darlin'. This stallion is more than a little frisky—care to break him in?'

'Actually, no, I was hoping for a wild ride.'

His brows shot up.

She walked towards him, letting her hips sway. 'Ever done that, Daniel? Ever totally given up control? Ever just done what you wanted regardless of how crazy just because it felt too good not to?'

'I thought I did that last night.'

'I think you can do better.'

'Do you now?'

'Maybe. Can you, Daniel? Forget everything but how you feel? Can you *not* think? That enough of a challenge for you?'

'*Not think?* Trouble, if I was thinking, I wouldn't be here right now.'

Her mouth softened in appreciation. If she were thinking she'd be out of here too. Instead the feeling was too good to ignore. 'Dance with me.'

He took her in waltz hold and expertly span her around the room. She pushed him away, waggling her finger at him as if he were a naughty schoolboy. 'You're still in control, Daniel. I want you to lose it.'

He pulled her closer. 'You know, you're not that great at letting go either, Lucy. You're too busy coming up with cutting comments and being all prickly.'

She stared up at him. There were reasons for the prickles. Good ones. Protective ones.

His eyes accused her. 'You don't want anyone to get too close.'

Well, he was as guilty of that as she was. And, yeah, she

found it hard to trust people. Now the person she trusted least was herself. She wanted Daniel beyond belief but he couldn't give her anything more than his body—and even that was only on short-term loan, so she had to do the protective thing more than ever.

'Ever let go, Lucy? Ever not think?' This wasn't right—he wasn't supposed to turn the tables.

'On the dance floor.'

'OK.' Wicked light flared in his eyes. 'Dance *for* me.'

She stepped back from him, her smile of delight wide as she figured the way to rule him again. 'You want me to strip too?'

'I…um…'

The key to success—she'd just rendered him speechless. Out of control was fast approaching, for both of them. She shimmied towards him. 'I'm dancing to country, you know, in my head.'

'As I can't hear it, that's just fine.'

She spent the night in his arms. Sleeping with him. All night. Relaxed. Secure. Everything she'd wanted, from the wrong man—the emotional vacuum that was Daniel Graydon. Fate was nasty.

He rose early. From his bed she watched through the open door as he shaved and showered. He walked back through. Silent. She could see he was miles away, no doubt already mentally slugging it out in the courtroom. He dressed. Dark suit, white shirt, dark tie. Her passionate, playful lover disappeared under the guise, turned into a frowning figure. Austere. She hated it.

Then he surprised her by turning to her with a smile that made her forget his clothing. 'Walk with me. Come and see where I work.'

She didn't want to. She really didn't want to. 'Why?'

He shrugged. 'Why not? A walk in the early-morning sun will do you some good.'

She slipped from the bed and pretended to ignore the growing glitter in his eyes as she stepped into her jeans.

'Do you always go commando?'

She grinned and shook her head.

'I'm not sure I believe you. Every time I tell you to get dressed you don't bother with underwear.'

'It's the rebel in me. I'm doing as asked but not all the way. My little act of defiance.'

He chuckled. 'Yeah. That figures.'

Daniel had left all the files at the office to be brought over by his team so, other than his briefcase, he was unburdened on the walk. They called into the café and got coffee to go.

'You don't want food?' Lucy asked.

'Maybe later,' he answered distractedly.

She swiped a banana from the bowl on the counter and added it to her purchase.

As they headed into lawyerville Lucy's feeling of intimidation grew. Insecure, threatened, she thought she saw everyone looking her way. Conscious of her ancient jeans and less-than-fresh top, she had a needy moment. 'They probably think I'm one of your clients.'

'Probably,' Daniel answered carelessly.

He stopped walking and turned to her, briefcase in one hand while the other lifted to her face. Then he combed his fingers through her hair, cupping the back of her head and pulling her close. The kiss was sweltering. Hot, hungry, open. No restraint. His briefcase hit the ground as his other hand slipped beneath the waistband of her jeans and curved around her bare buttock, squeezing gently. Just as suddenly it was over.

She snaked in a breath and wished they were miles away from here. Together, alone and naked.

Daniel grinned at her. 'Now they don't.'

She glanced around the group of lawyers. Saw them swapping stunned looks.

'You're a bad influence on me, Lucy.'

'Why's that?'

'You have me liking to shock people.'

She handed him the banana. 'To keep your energy up.'

He took it with a smile and went to join his team.

Not liking the way he fitted in so perfectly with them she turned and walked—fast, almost smacking straight into Sarah.

'Hello, Lucy.' She had a frozen smile pinned to her face and icicles in her eyes. Lucy knew she wasn't cutting the mustard as far as Sarah was concerned. She knew Sarah had seen that shattering kiss. She'd looked shocked, though not half as shocked as Lucy.

The day passed in a haze. Lucy went to work in the early afternoon and did some more on her proposal—the one she'd give to Lara on her return. She had some ideas about taking the club to the next level and ached to be given the chance to do it. She liked nothing more than hanging out there. It was second only to the time in Daniel's bed. She was filled with desires she'd never expected to experience. Wanting to work. Wanting to love.

Late afternoon and punters arrived. Isabel clocked on to help with the post-work rush. Lucy smiled at the regulars she was getting to know well. She was actually content.

Daniel appeared late in the evening. She'd been wondering how he'd got on, and worrying about the hours he worked. Hell. She was turning into his mother. He sat at the end of the bar—his usual seat—and ordered a whiskey. She felt his eyes on her, watching her every move as she poured the drink. She set it in front of him but said nothing, sensing his need for space. So she moved about the bar, serving patrons, chatting with Isabel, clearing glasses and all the while intensely aware of him as he sat and sipped and stared after her.

He looked wired. He should be home asleep. She wondered what was going on in that brain of his. She knew the trouble he had in shutting it down. Eventually she could take it no longer. Telling Isabel she was taking a break, she went to the end of the bar, took hold of his hand and pulled. He stood and let her lead him behind the bar to the back office. She closed and locked the door.

He went ahead and sat on the sofa, watching as she moved towards him, purpose explicit. His lips curled in anticipation. She slipped her panties off, leaving her skirt on, and unbuttoned her black satin blouse so her bra was revealed. She said nothing. Didn't need to.

She straddled him, stroked his face with her fingertips, easing the hard planes of his jaw. He sat rapt. She leant forward to tease his lips with the tips of her nipples. Her breathing and pulse accelerated as his tongue darted.

His hand slid beneath her skirt. 'I love it when you're like this.' His fingers teased her. 'Can I…?'

'You can do anything you want.'

Licence to thrill—her. And he soon had her spiralling out of control. She shook her head, breathless, close to climax. 'I wasn't meaning for this…'

His grin was lazy. 'I like making you come. Watching you. Tasting you. Hearing you.'

But she wasn't going to let it all be her. She pulled at his clothing—enough to get to him. Grasping, her hand rubbed in time to her own rhythm. Faster and harder as her body contracted.

'Let me in.' He groaned. 'I need to be in now.'

His jaw was stubbled; his troubled eyes burnt into her. She slipped on the protection and slid him home, then set the pace. Slow to start, she watched him, waiting for the moment when his eyes went glassy and sensation took over, switching off his mind, making his body his master—only interested in and able to feel. Then she began to stoke the heat, pumping him harder, faster. Knew she was succeeding when every single one of those hundred or so muscles beneath her tautened and his breath came harsh. His arms came about her tighter. One hand twisting in her hair, the other at her waist, pulling her closer.

'Lucy…' He groaned her name as his hips jerked up towards

her, faster and faster, and her head fell back as he pulled on her hair. He kissed her neck, nipping at it as he worked the pressure out in a frantic rhythm. And she delighted in it—satisfaction pouring through as they broke free of the tension together.

Finally she felt him relax. She whispered, 'You should go home and sleep.'

'No.'

'You have a big day tomorrow.'

'I'm not leaving here without you.'

They said nothing on the late walk home. He led her into the shower and then to his bed where they tumbled together in the cool cotton sheets. She lay beside him in the pre-dawn hours—awake but not unhappy. She studied his face in repose. It was a relief in a way not to have those penetrating eyes focused on her—trying to search out all her secrets while guarding his own.

His arm tightened around her, his brow furrowed. He jerked awake.

'Hell.' He stared at her, then stared at the digital clock. He swore more sharply. Casting her an amazed look, he slid from the bed. 'I slept in!'

She glanced at the clock—ten past seven didn't seem like that much of a sleep-in, but knowing Daniel he'd have been at the pool powering it out for an hour by now.

Daniel strode to work, breathing deeply to blow the webs out of his sleep-mussed head. The case was to resume at ten. Crazily, despite the fact he'd had more sleep than usual, he was tired. But he'd been tired before and knew adrenalin would get him through the day. It would make his mind crystal-clear.

What wasn't at all clear was what was happening with him and that crazy woman. He thought of the other night. She'd been the one teasing off her clothes but he was the one who'd been stripped. She'd seized control and made him lose his. Pushing him, exposing him, until he'd reached out with both hands and taken her like a man possessed. Inner demons and deepest desires unleashed. Wanting her utterly. Holding her tight to him. And she had revelled in it, leading him to repeat the indulgence.

Time and time she welcomed him in with hot, sweet fervour. The way her core contracted around him, the way she gazed at him with such intense honesty until she could bear it no longer, the way her fingers curled into his hair, an instinctive reflex as her body shook in pleasure…

He wanted her. And the more he had of her, the more he wanted.

It wasn't supposed to work that way. It was supposed to have the opposite effect. He should be getting cured, not more highly infected with the Lucy bug.

He looked at his schedule. He was double-booked again. How was he supposed to give a talk at the law school at the same time the Judge was due to sum up? He checked his emails. The Law Society wanted him to prepare a paper. He glanced at his in-tray—neat, orderly, but still overflowing. Time. He didn't have time to do all of this and he wanted to. And now he felt as if there was more he wanted. She'd done something to him, made him feel as if he was missing out. He pulled paper towards him in irritation. Missing out on what? He didn't want or need someone warming his bed at night. He would not, could not, become dependent on anyone—least of all her.

She'd told him from the start she didn't stick around any place for long and he knew too well the bitter taste of abandonment. He'd witnessed his father's descent into an insular, workaholic world once his mother had walked out. Daniel too had been lacerated by her lack of interest—her lack of love for a son who'd been stupid enough to believe in the whole 'happy family' thing. He'd never risk being that vulnerable again, certainly never make the same mistake as his father and rely on another like that.

He was having a fly-by fling with Lucy. That was all. Not a relationship. Relationships always ended.

But her presence in his home threatened his peace. His carefully built life was starting to crumble—there were gaps where there should be walls. And Lucy was the one holding the sledgehammer.

He was going to have to get rid of her.

CHAPTER ELEVEN

You believe justice is more important than mercy

LUCY read the article again and again. As she sat in the café the pleasantness of the warm sunny morning passed her by. She stared at that morning's paper—at the photo of Daniel looking every inch the aggressive lawyer in black and white. She marched back to his apartment, watched the television, surfed the Internet and even put on the radio for the national news station. Her blood began to boil as Daniel's questions were quoted. Footage showed him striding out of the courthouse, stopping to address the media briefly on behalf of his client. Hotshot lawyer in defence mode shredding the complainant's argument. It hit every mutinous button within her. She knew she shouldn't have got involved with a guy like him.

Daniel climbed the stairs of the club with a feeling of extreme relief, completely forgetting his resolve to end it with her, he was so exhausted. All he knew was that in a few moments he'd be able to leave the case behind—just sit on his stool at the bar and watch her and relax in a way he'd never been able to before. He could hardly wait. Her eyes met his the minute he walked in and he knew she'd been waiting for him. But he didn't get that wide, devilish smile. Instead she looked away again—fast. Something was up. He took his seat under the light. The one that was always empty because everyone knew it was his.

She banged the glass down in front of him, grabbed the whiskey and poured it in with a heavy hand, some of it sloshing over the rim to the bar below.

'Actually I didn't fancy a whiskey tonight.'

'Really? Fine.'

To his utter amazement she picked up the glass and downed the contents in one gulp.

She hissed fire.

'Call me astute, but I'm guessing something's bothering you.'

'You think?' She banged the glass down. 'What gives you that idea?'

He moved the glass out of her reach. 'I don't think we need any more accidents.'

'No. We don't. We don't need anything more of anything.'

Daniel sighed inwardly. She was clearly spoiling for a fight, clearly choosing him as the opponent and, frankly, he couldn't be bothered. 'Look, Trouble, I'm not in the mood for figuring out what's going on in your convoluted mind this evening, so if you have a problem just spit it out.'

'My problem, Counsellor, is your case.'

'You sound like you're in a bad American legal drama. What do you mean, my case?'

'What are you doing defending that creep?'

Daniel's attention focused. OK. So this wasn't personal. It was professional. Interesting. She wanted to argue about the case?

'Creep?'

'Yeah, the jerk who spiked that woman's drink and then assaulted her.'

'Ever heard of a thing called "presumption of innocence"?'

'He's not innocent.'

'I didn't realise you were judge and jury.'

'Hmmf,' she growled. Her hands shook. She was in a right rage. 'Why are you defending him?'

'Because I happen to believe he's innocent. And even if it's proved he isn't, he's entitled to good representation.'

'By good you mean resourceful. Get him off on some technicality…or look for some legal loophole, some procedural slip-up that renders half the evidence inadmissible?'

Daniel blinked, in a bit of a headspin. 'No, I—'

She didn't let him finish. 'And what about the victim? You put her on the stand and tear shreds off her, right? Pry into her personal life? Cast shadows and doubt?'

'Lucy, I…' *have had a really long day and don't need this.* But one look at her face and he knew he needed to straighten this out. He'd seen her cross, he'd seen her excited, but he'd never seen her looking hurt before—never this agitated. He didn't like it.

'Ever been a victim, Daniel? Ever known what it's like to have someone come in and screw over your life?'

'No. But…' *I'm guessing you have.* He bit the words back. She was distressed, something must have happened and he wanted to understand, not upset her more. He stood, took her arm and marched her towards the office. 'I think we need to continue this in private.'

She didn't argue. Just pulled her arm roughly from his and stalked ahead into the room. He could hardly believe this was the woman who had launched on him in lust last night. She stood as far from him as possible. Arms barred tight across her body. 'It's so unfair. What woman would put herself through that—through the trial, have her life paraded in front of everyone—if he wasn't guilty?'

He spoke calmly, quietly. 'I have no doubt that something happened to her. What I doubt is whether they've caught the right guy.'

'There's a witness saying he was there.'

'Him and half the city. There might be another explanation. Look, Lucy, my guy isn't Snow White, but his line is burglary and car theft, not sexual assault. He's not the sharpest tool in the box—he doesn't have the smarts to pull something like this one off.'

'Yeah, right.'

'He was in the wrong place at the wrong time. The cops got a match and patched the story together. It's not a strong case, they shouldn't have gone ahead with it because it's not fair on anyone—let alone the victim—but I'm not going to see an innocent man go to jail.'

His reasoning didn't stop her tirade. 'You lawyers are all the same. Only in it for the money. I remember the law students sauntering round campus like they owned it in their flash clothes, drinking their expensive wine, thinking they were so sophisticated.'

'Whoa, check out the size of that chip, Lucy. It's not about money. Not for me.' He had an inheritance. Money was never going to be an issue.

'Really?' she spat. 'Is he paying you a mint?'

'Actually he's paying me nothing.'

That shut her up—for a moment. 'You don't know what it's like. Victims don't have a voice.'

'Not true, Lucy. Not nowadays.'

'The system is geared towards the defendant. When it's he said versus she said, it seems like nine times out of ten they believe him.' She paced the tiny room. 'Are you putting him on the stand? Are you going to ask him all about his private life, his past, like you did her?'

'We have to test the credibility of the witness's evidence.'

'Hers, sure. What about his credibility? He doesn't have to get up there and face a scary inquisitor like you—she does. She's the one who's been through the wringer and you just make it worse. The bad guy gets to sit back and watch it all.'

'We're talking about a person's liberty, Lucy. We have to err on the side of caution. Beyond reasonable doubt.' Deliberately he kept his voice slow and low, forcing her to stop her pacing so she could hear him. Treating her as he would a fragile witness on the stand.

'What about *justice,* Daniel? Look at the stats—the bad guys hardly ever get put away. You know this—not unless you have some solid scientific evidence. They never believe her. It's always him.'

'So what would you have—anarchy? Vigilantes retaliating who knows how violently in their code of justice?'

She looked at her boots. 'Why don't we tie a rock to him and toss him in a lake? If he sinks he's telling the truth and if he floats he's lying? You know, that worked for all those witches a couple of hundred years ago, didn't it?'

He wanted to put his arms around her and cradle her—she was putting on the brave front but her eyes were over-shiny and her voice wobbled. 'We work within the system, Lucy. I'm not saying it's a perfect system, but it's not bad. If we work at it, we can make it even better.'

She kicked at the ground with her toe—grudging. Almost able to concede the point.

He made contact, looping his arms around her waist. 'Are we going to have a fight like this every time I take on a case you don't like?' He didn't know where that question had come from, but it was out now.

'No. It'll be more often than that because there's a lot we don't have in common.'

Amusement rumbled in him, making him forget the moment of panic over thinking of Lucy being around for more of his cases. He liked this challenge, liked her interest, the way her mind worked. 'I can think of one thing we have in common.' He slid his hands to her hips, but felt how stiff she stood in the loose embrace. She was too upset for fun right now, but he wanted to restore her peace. He sent soft strokes down her back with his palms and spoke as gently as he could in her ear. 'Are you going to tell me about it?'

Of course not! Lucy's hackles spiked. She was never going to tell him about the worst night of her life. The night that had damned her self-confidence, cemented her 'waste of space' reputation and left her thinking maybe the world was right and she'd never amount to anything much. She never spoke about it. She never wanted to think about it.

Yet here she was, thinking and thinking and wanting rid of it for once and for all.

Impossible.

For long moments they stood silent. He didn't ask again. Didn't press the point. But she knew he was waiting. The gentle rhythm of his hands had a soothing, almost soporific effect. She felt herself slipping, his patience softening her, until resignation replaced tension. This was Daniel—he always got what he wanted. So, OK, she'd talk—a little. It wasn't really giving in. Besides, *she* suddenly wanted to. She wanted to lean on his unwavering, imperishable strength, just for a moment. Somehow he did this to her. Somehow she couldn't seem to deny him anything. But when she went to speak, anxiety knotted. It was little above a whisper.

'You'll think I'm even more of an idiot than you already do.'

'I'm not sure that's possible.' His teasing smile tickled. He lifted her chin so he could look into her eyes.

She ducked away, putting her forehead on his chest, not wanting him to see her humiliation. Not wanting his smile to disarm her further. But it was already too late—he only had to hold her like this and she'd do almost anything he asked.

'I was seventeen. Sneaked out of the school hostel to go clubbing.'

'Under-age Lucy.'

'Only just.' She sighed, unable to stop the flow now she'd started. 'And I was breaking all the school rules. My best friend from home was in the city for the weekend and we wanted to go dancing. Harmless enough.'

'What happened?'

'I'm not really sure. I'd been drinking cola—nothing added, nothing else. There were a couple of guys dancing near. Then things get a little confusing. I didn't feel so good. I went to go to the bathroom. Everything went kind of fuzzy and this guy asked me if I was OK, said something about getting me some fresh air.' She paused for breath. 'I just…went…' Her heart hit irregularly as she remembered. She skipped a bit. 'Sienna, my friend, came out of the club—she said I'd been gone about twenty minutes. She found me as I was being led down the street. She shouted and whoever it was with me ran and I fell…' She faltered again. 'The thing is I don't remember, Daniel. I don't remember what happened.'

He'd gone very still; she could feel the tenseness in the muscles that lay just beneath his skin. She struggled on, wanting to finish it. She hadn't spoken about this in so long and it was like breaking through a thick crust to get the words out. 'Sienna got me back to the school hostel, but I was so sick and my hands were all bloody from landing on the concrete. Matron appeared while I was trying to sneak in the door.'

'What did she do?'

'She thought I'd been drinking. Said I was making it up because I was scared of being in trouble for breaking out.'

'She didn't get you checked out?'

'This was Matron. She wasn't known for being understanding. And it wasn't the first time I'd been caught sneaking out.' She grimaced. 'But the next day I was still sick and she did get the doctor in.'

'And the doctor?'

'Believed me.' She nodded. 'Got the police to come and interview me.'

'You can't remember anything?'

'I remember him being close. Suffocating. And I couldn't push him away.'

Daniel stood unnaturally quiet, and she knew he was reining himself in. She pushed on.

'They asked me all sorts of horrible questions. I was seventeen, Daniel, and despite my appetite for going dancing I was an innocent seventeen and the doctor examined me and it was awful.'

She felt the tension stringing him out. 'Were you…?'

'Still innocent.' She remembered the relief she'd felt at that knowledge. She'd thought she was OK—had thought there would have to be some physical sign, some feeling, but to know for certain had been so good. But the experience of all those people drilling her with questions, judging her, made her feel stupid, as if she'd done something far worse than go for a dance. As if somehow she'd deserved it. She'd never liked the people who were in charge, but she had truly hated them from that moment on. And she'd been determined from then on never to be controlled by anyone or anything again.

She'd lost belief in herself, lost her faith in the system, and lost her trust in people. Especially men. She'd built up barriers, using her sarcasm, her attitude, as her protective prickles. Ever since she'd been unwilling to open up, to contemplate much in the way of relationships. She was Lucy, the foolish girl who'd never done particularly well with anything, why would anyone want more from her?

At least she knew where she stood with the man cradling her close now. Pretty much nowhere—just another casual fling. Long-term? Not likely.

And that, she told herself, she could handle, but before this ended she wanted some of his strength, wanted some of his brilliance, to rub off on her. She'd love to have just a fraction of the X-factor that meant everything he touched turned to gold.

But she was Lucy. And she was revealing her silly self with every word she spoke.

This was why she never spent more than a few months in any one job, or in any one place. Empty as it was at times. She wanted more, but felt as if people expected her to come up with sub-standard. She refused to respect those in authority because they had never respected her. And it was why she never spent the entire night in a man's arms—unable to trust enough to rest and relax. She refused to allow anyone to have the power to hurt her—her body, her heart.

But wasn't that happening right now? Daniel had her ceding that power. Somehow she slept with him—really slept. Somehow she trusted him. Somehow she'd just opened up to him—completely. Man, it scared her.

She forced herself to focus back to that awful time so she wouldn't panic over how vulnerable she was this very moment. Vehemence coloured her voice as she choked back the emotion. 'School mates looked at me sideways, stage whispers that I was meant to hear. That I was a slapper. And the thing is I wasn't, Daniel. Everyone thought I was this loose rebel and I wasn't. But the way they carried on made me realise how lucky I'd been that nothing much *had* happened. The courage it must take to get up there and give evidence. I wouldn't be brave enough to do it.'

'Yes, you would. You would if you had to.'

'No, I wouldn't. And what's the point? With hotshot lawyers like you out there able to destroy any credibility in a second—the girl who bunked off classes, barely scraping by. Making it all up because she didn't want to get in trouble or because she's attention-seeking.'

'Lucy.' He ran a finger down her cheek.

She pulled her head away, feeling ultra-defensive, regretting opening her mouth in the first place. 'I wasn't on a booze-and-boys bender. Or drugs.'

'Why did you sneak out?'

'I liked dancing. I liked the freedom. I hate being told what to do and when to do it all the time. It was just nice to get out and let my hair down—away from all the rules.' She sighed. 'Everything is so prescribed. Dictated. I need a little bit of leeway, you know?'

A puff of amusement escaped him. 'Yes. I know.'

'Well, when you've spent your life being told what to do and when to do it you can't help but rebel. My father had us like performing monkeys. You should meet my sister.'

'Why?'

'She got the brunt of it. I think after a while he realised he wasn't going to get a golden girl in me, so he hounded her. But with him at home and then the screws at boarding-school…' She tilted her head, stretching out the strain in her neck muscles. 'I don't like to be locked up, Daniel.'

He laughed. 'Not many people do.'

'No, and I do like to have fun.'

There was a silence, he held her loosely and she began to soften. 'It wasn't your fault, Lucy.' He spoke softly but her tension flooded back. That was the thing—the self-blame. If only she'd done this, if only she hadn't done that…

He gave her a gentle shake. 'It could have happened to anyone.'

She failed to reply, knowing in her head he was right, but unable to stop the feeling he was wrong. She felt fated to fail—always to be the one in the wrong place at the wrong time. Never quite getting it right. Never quite good enough.

'So this happened, yet you work in bars?'

'I like seeing people out having a good time. I like helping them have a good time. Welcoming them, making the environment fun.'

'But things like drinks-spiking probably happen all the time.'

Her inner fighter finally limbered up. 'Why should I let one creep ruin something I love doing? I love going dancing—millions of us women do. And maybe, just maybe, I can run a tighter ship and stop it happening so much.'

'How?'

'Encourage women to drink direct from a bottle with a straw.' She answered fast and flippant, cracking a smile for the first time. 'Seriously. It's harder to slip anything into.'

He smiled back and it made her forget she'd been feeling mad at him. 'You see, you are brave, Lucy. You are doing something. You get back out there and take them on. You'd go to court if you ever had to. Piece of cake.'

'No, that's different. That's having your life ripped up by arrogant jerks like—' She broke off.

'Like me.' He grimaced. 'That's not how it is.'

'Yes, it is.' She felt sadness. 'There has to be a better way.'

'This is why you don't want to like me.'

Ouch, he was astute. She bit her lip. 'It's not you. It's what you stand for. I see a guy like you so bright, so talented, and you're on *his* side.'

'It's not about sides, Lucy.'

'Yes, it is. You know it is. It all comes down to who has the better lawyer. Who is the jury more likely to listen to?'

'If it bothers you that much, why don't you do something about it?'

'Like what? I wouldn't know where to start. But you could, Daniel. You have that brain, you have the knowledge and training and smarts to fix things.'

He laughed. 'That's flattering, but…' He shook his head. 'I can't change the world, Lucy, but I can maybe change one person's world.'

'No, you can do more than that, Daniel. You can.'

'You're talking about a dilemma that's been debated for years now.'

'Yeah, but you could do it—I know you could. If someone like you doesn't try, what hope is there for the rest of us?' She stared up at him, her eyes searching his, seeing the clarity there in the brown-gold. The brightness in the depths that had her so smitten.

He stared back, unusually silent. He cocked his head. 'Are you saying you believe in me, Lucy?'

'Yep. Super powers all the way.' She rolled her eyes and tried to act as if she'd meant it totally sarcastic.

He chuckled. But his hand reached out and he brushed his knuckles across her cheek. 'Thank you.' He spoke softly and smiled.

Oh, dear. Things were going from bad to worse. She was slipping from waist-deep to well over her head. She wanted him and with him like this she wanted even more—like everything. Stupid, because he didn't have it to give—he'd told her that right at the start. She looked away. 'I'm sorry. You don't need all this. You're in the middle of a case and have enough to be getting on with without me banging on about something that happened years ago.' She opened her mouth to blether on some more and apologise and try to make light of it, but he stopped her with a finger on her lips.

She stilled, suddenly hit by an unexpected and heady relief from unburdening her load. It mixed with the need to get physical. She should stick to physical with Daniel. Anything more muddied the waters and she was in enough danger of drowning in his magic as it was.

"Don't." He ran his finger across her lips, tracing their outline. She fought hard not to touch it with her tongue—desire was kicking high. 'Will you let me do something?'

'Um. OK.' Please let it be lust-related. Please let them get back to mindless.

'Let me take you home, let me hold you, so we can sleep—like we did last night.'

Her eyes closed, blinking for a second longer than usual in relief and in anticipation of security. In those precious moments when Daniel was beside her, inside her, all feeling of inadequacy fled. All thought fled—especially the nagging doubt. It was one thing he could offer her, and fool that she was, she'd take it gladly.

In his apartment he didn't bother with lights, just kept hold of her hand and led her straight to his room. With gentle arms that soon became passionate he held her close to him, stroked and kissed her body as if it were the most precious thing. He saved his own release until he was certain she'd had hers and then some. And eventually she was too tired to figure the confusion.

Feeling at peace, he heard her breathing regulate and deepen—she was asleep. He glanced at the neon light of his digital clock—his nemesis. Ordinarily minutes passed like hours as he suffered through his usual sleeplessness. Only tonight it wasn't such a struggle because he had her to hold. He relaxed and let his mind wander. She'd been so angry this evening, and had made some good points. Evidence was an area that interested him a lot. How to make the law better, the judicial system fairer. He frowned as he thought about her experience. His body tightened. Someone had tried to hurt her and she'd been hurt far worse by the people who should have been protecting her. So now, she'd developed a mouthy shell as her defence. He wanted to breach that defence—wanted to be let in to the vibrant warmth she had inside.

Irritated by his pathetic obsessing over her, he concentrated on the career decisions he'd have to make in the near future. Courtroom versus lecture theatre. His father wanted him to be partner and women like Sarah were attracted to his status. But success at work didn't equate with success in relationships. Look at his father—a stellar career and yet it still hadn't been enough to keep his mother happy.

He circled back to Lucy. She didn't care much for what he did, but she seemed to have an unshakeable faith in his ability—and in him. That both touched and terrified him. Yet she didn't expect anything from him herself. She just wanted him, as he was.

Smiling into the darkness, he relived some of those moments of want. He must have drifted off because it was relatively late again when he woke. She was the one to sleep in this time. She was using his chest as her pillow, her hair draping over it, her warm breath fanning over his chest. He was careful not to move, not wanting to disturb her.

Her hand rested on his stomach and he concentrated really hard on not getting too hard because he wanted her to have as much sleep as she could before the time would come when he'd have to slip away. That would wake her and he knew she wouldn't get back to sleep after that. Then he noticed her hand was sliding south, to his lower abdomen, and he figured his effort might be wasted—she wasn't asleep at all any more.

'Lucy,' he said, unable to get his voice louder than a whisper as her head began to follow the direction of her hand, her mouth pressing kisses in a line directly down. She brushed her hair back behind her ear so he was able to see her face in profile as she moved down the bed, moved down on him. Anticipation shook through him as she licked her lips. He clenched the sheet—and his teeth, the sigh whistling through them as she took him in her mouth.

Half of him wanted to keep staring, watching her beautiful mouth and beautiful hair wrap round him, while the other half wanted to close his eyes and descend into an almost semi-conscious state so he could just focus on the way she made him feel and the way she felt.

What a way to wake up.

CHAPTER TWELVE

You enjoy the challenge of competition

EARLY afternoon Lucy polished the beer taps as a displacement activity. Mindless. She was not going to think about what on earth was going on between her and Daniel. For the first time in her life she felt better about her past. He'd listened. He'd reasoned. And she'd slipped even more under his spell. She was dangerously close to equating spectacular sex with latent love. Although her feelings for him were growing less than latent and more like lethal. She'd told him she wasn't stupid, but she was starting to suspect otherwise. She'd have to be, to fall for Daniel. Mr Never Ever Committing.

She was not going to panic.

Ah, hell. Who was she kidding? Her heart pounded at double speed every moment. Trying to figure him out, not trying to figure them out—it was exhausting. Sarah walked into the bar. Lucy tensed, not sure what Sarah could want. Quite certain she didn't want to know. But she could bluff her way through it—make as if she didn't mind whatever the woman had to say. 'I thought you'd still be in court.'

'Daniel is. He doesn't need me.'

Lucy stared but refrained from making the comment that leapt to mind. 'Right. Well, can I help you somehow?'

'A chardonnay would be nice.'

'Sure.'

She went to the fridge and got a bottle.

'You want one?'

'No, thanks, I'm working.'

'Yes.' Sarah gave the bar a scathing glance. 'Daniel said you did music at university.'

'Mmm hmm.' What was he doing discussing her—especially with Sarah?

'You didn't want to play in an orchestra?'

'I'm not good enough,' Lucy said boldly. 'I only did music because my best friend was and I needed to pick something. It's not really a great passion or talent of mine.'

The slightly startled look in Sarah's eyes gave some satisfaction. But clearly the woman was here to belittle her so Lucy decided to make a clean breast of it and do it all by herself. 'I waitressed my way through the holidays and when I finished my second-rate degree I fell into waitressing full-time.' She poured Sarah's wine and then picked up another glass to polish.

'So you've been working as a barmaid since you graduated.'

Lucy momentarily stopped wiping the glass. 'With time off for slacking around, yeah.'

'Well, they do say opposites attract, I guess.'

'Meaning?'

'You and Daniel. You're not exactly alike, are you?' She leant forward as if they were sharing confidences in a girly chat. 'Daniel's going places. Places I'm not sure you're aware of, Lucy.'

'Oh? How interesting. Do tell.' She smiled, feeling her cheeks pinch with the effort of pulling them back.

'He's targeted as the next partner for the firm, the university is chasing him to lecture there and there's even talk of him being one of the youngest to be appointed to the bench.'

'As in be a judge?'

Sarah nodded. 'He needs a partner who can keep pace with him. Who can hold her own in that society.' She wrinkled her nose at the wine and set it down again, not sipping. 'He has a lot to decide in the next while—which direction he's going to go in. He needs a woman who can help him make that right decision.'

'I'm thrilled to know he has such a glittering future ahead of him. Makes him all the more attractive, don't you think?' Lucy held the glass up to the light and looked at it as if it were some cut-crystal masterpiece worth hundreds. 'I'm such a lucky girl, aren't I? But as for helping him with his decisions, well, you know, Daniel's a big boy.' She paused for effect. 'I'm sure he can figure it out for himself.'

'I'm quite sure he will, Lucy. But you wouldn't want his options limited because his wife wasn't able to hold her own.'

Wife?

Lucy held back the laugh with a mental vice. The woman was way off-key. But frankly she was so horrible, Lucy didn't want to make her feel any better. Wife? She and Daniel were having a no-holds-barred sex-a-thon for no apparent reason other than that it felt good. So good. And they got more sleep as a result.

She already knew she was way out of Daniel's league. She didn't need lawyer-lady ramming it even further down her gagging throat. But there was nothing more to it, not for him anyway. They'd fully admitted they were totally wrong for each other. He'd be bored soon enough and she'd hit the road and mend her heart in private. But she certainly wasn't going to leave him for this calculating monster to try to get her hands on. They lived in New Zealand in the twenty-first century. There wasn't supposed to be a class system. Snobbery of that sort wasn't supposed to happen here. Although, she grimaced, remembering the shocked-looking stares of the other lawyers outside the courthouse when Daniel had kissed her, maybe the legal fraternity was a little more conservative than most.

He'd even admitted he'd liked using her to shock. It was all just a bit of fun for him. Crossing the wire, doing something a little different or unexpected—for a while. He'd laugh about it in years to come—*I once had this flaming affair with this drifter muso—she was a flake but good in the sack. I spent more time in bed with her than I ever did usually. She was a convenience—that's all.*

She knew she wasn't being fair, but she couldn't help it.

She wasn't even a musician—not any more. When was the last time she'd opened her violin case? Not once since bumping into Daniel in the agency that afternoon.

And Daniel a judge? If he were appointed his life would be different. He'd be a pillar of society—scrupulous. A little reserved, distanced from the general population—not too far from how he was now. So, no, he couldn't be married to a girl who served up pints for the local clubbers. Not good enough.

Married. Ha.

She'd take what she could get from him—until she decided it was time to move on. Until they heard from Lara. When Lara came back she'd hit the road. Until then she could keep a handle on it, couldn't she? Not lose her heart in the process.

Meantime she was not going to let this woman make her feel inferior with a stab here and a twist of a knife there. She was not going to let it bother her at all. Quickly she sifted through her CDs and rammed one in, selecting the track. As Sarah left the bar, her wine untouched, the strains of Tammy Wynette's classic sang out—'Stand By Your Man.'

The minute Sarah had gone Lucy called to Corey that he was on his own for a couple of hours. She needed to get out and think. She had the itch and was starting to wish she could skip out. Things were getting just that little bit too complicated.

She got back to the bar just after four p.m., having almost walked the heels off her boots, and was amazed when she saw Daniel there. In casual—well, as casual as Daniel got—navy linen shirt, sleeves rolled back, bending over the pool cue apparently in a duel with Corey. His bottom half was clad in jeans. *Jeans.* In the middle of the afternoon.

Lucy walked straight over to him. 'Where's your white shirt?'

'I gave a lunchtime lecture at the university today. Figured I didn't need it.'

'And now you're following through on the student thing and bunking the afternoon to go to a bar?'

'I've taken the afternoon off.'

'You're kidding.'

He grinned. 'Four jury members are down with food poisoning and everyone's excused until tomorrow. So I made it to the lecture in time. I've done enough for today.'

She looked him over. 'Lecture popular?'

'Good crowd, yeah.'

Full house, she bet. 'Lots of girls? Front row? Looking gorgeous?'

A small smile. She gave him the once-over again. He did the 'handsome young professor' look well. Too well.

'What—you think they weren't there to hear me talk?'

'Oh, I'm quite sure they were hanging on your every word.'

Lucy leaned against a table nearby and watched as Daniel played the shots. The final shots—he sank the black in style.

Corey groaned. 'Aw, man, I thought you said you didn't play much.'

Daniel grinned, putting the pool cue aside. 'Just lucky, I guess.'

Yeah, right. 'Are you good at everything you do?' Man, it irritated her. That he could turn his hand to anything and master it—excel, in fact, just like that. Why wasn't talent shared around normal people?

He smiled at her snap. 'You tell me. Am I good?'

She glared. 'You know you are.'

'You game to take me on, then?' He nodded towards the table.

She had already taken him on that table in a far more serious game than she was willing to admit and he was winning at that hands down. She shook her head. 'I have to work.'

'You're working too hard.' He followed her over to the bar.

'Rich coming from you.'

'I'm serious. The hours you're working are too long.'

She cupped her hands around her mouth like a pretend megaphone. 'Pot calling kettle, come in, kettle.'

'I'm used to it.'

Meaning she wasn't? Thanks very much. Despite knowing he was right it annoyed her. He thought she was a flake. Not up to the job, unable to sustain and maintain a decent work ethic. 'Yeah. Well. Life'll pass you by.'

He cocked his head and studied her, abandoning Corey's suggestion of a best-of-three competition. 'What's up?'

'Your friend was in here earlier.'

'Friend?'

'Yeah, the woman you work with. What's her name—' she showed her deep-in-thought face '—um...?'

'Sarah?'

'Yes, that's it. Sarah.'

His eyes were dancing and she knew her pretence at forgetting the witch's name was as bad an acting job as you could get.

'What did Sarah have to say?'

'Oh, she was full of your future.'

His brows shot up. 'My future?'

Lucy nodded. 'Apparently you're the man, Daniel. Partner, professor, even a judge if the rumours are to be believed.'

He nodded slowly. 'Yes, I'm next up for a full partnership and the dean of the law faculty called me in this afternoon. There's a position coming up.' He grinned. 'I think the judge thing is a little premature.'

Yeah, but he wasn't denying it was a possibility.

She filled her trusty red bottle with water from the postmix and tried not to remember his torso in the sodden shirt from that night. That was the trouble with the postmix these days—every time she went to use it, she thought of him. She frowned at it.

'Why was Sarah talking about that with you?'

'Oh, I don't know. It just came up in passing.' She decided not to totally backstab the woman. He had to work with her. And if he had one of his two-date flings with her, what did Lucy care? She'd have left town and forgotten all about him.

Her frown deepened.

'You don't find talking about my career fascinating?' he teased.

She glanced up. 'Oh, no. It's interesting. You've worked really hard to get to where you are. It's pretty amazing.'

He shrugged. 'Life isn't all about good grades.'

'It is for you.'

'You're not as much of a slacker as you like to make out.' He pulled her up. 'You didn't scrape by, Lucy—you went to university, you got a degree. You're not a drop-out.'

'That was only because of Sienna—my best friend. We got into music together. It was a hobby, an excuse to go into her garage—supposedly to practise but more to hang and chat. A way of getting away from my parents.'

'I guess I was lucky finding what I wanted to do early on. It was always law for me.' He drummed his fingers on the bar. 'Have you never had something you're passionate about? That you eat, breathe and sleep?'

She had something now. Something she really wanted to excel at—could excel at. Two things, in fact. How was it she'd finally found what she was meant to do, and the man she was meant to do it all with, and it be so, so wrong? She could never, ever share it with him. It wasn't something he was capable of. He was too busy serving a higher purpose.

He took her silence as a negative.

'What about your violin?'

'What about it? It was a hobby taken too far. My heart was never in it—you can hear it in my playing.'

'You love country music, though.'

'Yeah.' She chuckled. 'But that's just for fun. Ever heard Bach played country-style?'

'Can't say I have.'

'I'll do it for you later.'

'There's only one way you'll get me listening to you playing country.'

'How?'

'Naked. Naked country-music playing.'

'Naked?' Her shriek caused customers three tables away to turn to them.

He relented. 'Oh, OK. You can wear your cowgirl boots.'

She swatted him with the bar towel and played out the mock outrage a little more. She was secretly turned on by the whole idea but annoyed because she knew he read her mind. He lazily took his seat at the end of the bar and toyed with his drink, chatting idly to Corey about who was top of the table in the rugby.

Lucy kept staring at him out of the corner of her eye. She'd never seen him so relaxed. Daniel doing down time was even more attractive than Daniel doing single-minded obsessive.

It was only halfway through the evening when he called to her, devilish temptation in his face. 'Come home. Leave Corey to finish up tonight.'

'Just because you're having a night off doesn't mean the rest of us don't have to work.'

He was more dangerous tonight than she'd known him to be these entire two weeks. And her heart was doing dangerous pittery-pattery, skittery moves.

'Don't worry about it. Corey can handle it.'

'No, really, Daniel. I have to work. You go on ahead of me.' She jerked her head to the door.

He looked put out. Because he expected her to put out every time he fancied it? She decided the fact she fancied it too was irrelevant because for her it was way more than lust—more than just a physical relief to bring dreamless nights. She was starting to dream—impossible dreams. He was in the premier division; she was on the reserve bench of the Z-grade. Sarah's words had left a little welt that was now festering, and the infection was spreading. She could never keep him. She could never keep up with him—she'd only hold him back.

'You're spending too much time here. You never did have that night off I ordered.' So he wasn't taking no for an answer. 'Corey—you lock up!' Corey spun round from where he'd been clearing a table and the tray of glasses he had in his hands slipped—glass shattering everywhere.

Lucy couldn't stop the giggle as she tried to tell Daniel off. 'You should never have done that.'

He flashed her a wicked smile. 'I'll sign it off. Come on, let's go have some fun.'

Casual Daniel wanted to play. And that was a Daniel she couldn't refuse.

CHAPTER THIRTEEN

You rely on reason rather than intuition

DANIEL got back from court—and a not guilty verdict—to find the dean of the law school had been trying to contact him all morning. He rang him back right away and was offered the job. Even though he'd been expecting it, the rush of satisfaction hit hard.

He pushed away from his desk and stood—went out of the office and told his secretary he was going for a walk.

'Daniel, you're supposed to be meeting Miles for lunch.'

'Cancel it.'

The stunned expression on her face made him relent. 'Apologise profusely. Tell him I'm not feeling well.'

His life was getting way too complicated. He headed to the outdoor pool. He always thought things through in the water, but today he couldn't settle into his stroke. He abandoned the attempt and went for the walk he'd said he was going to. Somehow he ended up along by the club. He didn't go in. Didn't want Lucy thinking he was coming to gloat over his verdict. He could hardly go in high-fiving. He wanted to play that one carefully. A lot of what she'd said was right. There were no real winners today.

Immediately on his return to the office he was called in to his managing partner. The one he'd ditched at lunch.

Miles leapt to his feet as soon as he saw him. 'It's time we had that talk, Daniel. More than time.'

'You know the university has made me an offer.' It was a confirmation of knowledge, not a question.

'I knew they wanted to. I can understand it. You've got a brilliant brain for research and your enthusiasm for the law is palpable. You can make the most complex law crystal-clear to the most uneducated Joe on the jury and as a lecturer you'll have students captivated. But you're also a sight in the courtroom, Daniel. That's your home. We can give you the resources you need. We know other firms have tried to headhunt you. You've stuck with us and we want to reward that, by promoting you to full partner. You're the youngest we've ever made the offer to.' He smiled. 'There are substantial benefits, of course.'

Daniel knew. Remuneration the university could never compete with. But then the university had other kinds of benefits—holidays, for one. Sabbaticals. Time to research and write.

'I know you like to do a lot—pro bono, lectures for law school and the Law Society. All good stuff and good for the firm, but you have to be sure you can fully commit to us.'

That word. Commit. He'd been skating around it for some time.

'I'm sure you'll think it through with your usual precision.'

Daniel nodded and exited. Satisfied but still hungry. You'd think he'd be happy with all his pigeons coming to roost. This was what he'd been working towards for the last eight years. Setting up his pick. Trouble was, now he had to choose and he didn't know where to start.

He knocked on his father's door having bypassed the usual necessary appointment. For once in his life he needed his father to be a father, not a mentor. Managing partner at Graydon Jefferies, he'd been disappointed that Daniel hadn't followed him into the commercial law arena and made it Graydon & Son. But for Daniel sealing deals and clinching contracts around the world wasn't really law. It was the cut and thrust of the courtroom battle he liked. The testing of evidence and the theoretical development of the law in which society operated that got him going. Not sorting out matters between large, already wealthy firms. He chuckled under his breath. Lucy was right; he was an idealist.

'Hi, son. How is it?'

Daniel knew he was referring to his work and nothing else. 'Good.'

'You're lecturing at the university again, I see.'

Daniel nodded.

'Don't hang out with all those academics too much though, will you? Get back to your ace-lawyer act in the courtroom. You'll be a judge in no time.'

Did he want to be a judge?

'What about your caseload—still OK?'

Still crazy.

'Not still doing all that pro bono stuff, are you?'

Well.

'Partners won't be interested in that. You want to be a full partner, you bring in the money.'

Did he want to be a partner?

His father frowned. 'Although the publicity that last case brought was good.'

Daniel looked at his father another moment and wondered if he should mention Lucy. He figured there wasn't much point. His father went to bed with law tomes.

He stiffened. Up until a couple of weeks ago, so had he. Sure, he'd had his flings, but he'd still come back to his own bed, alone, with his books.

Now it wasn't enough. And for the first time he could understand his mother's side of his parents' relationship. As a youth he'd been angry with her for leaving—angry that she hadn't understood the drive that pushed his father, the ambition that he'd inherited. The desire to be the best, to make that difference. But looking around his father's opulent office he wasn't sure his father was interested in making a difference. He seemed more concerned about making money. Given there'd been money in the family going back generations, this seemed pointless.

Status. Was that why he pushed Daniel to aim to be the youngest partner? Or youngest judge? So he could bask in reflected glory? Daniel couldn't even be sure his father was happy. Sure, he had a successful career, but at the end of the day he went home to a house empty of everything except material possessions. He'd been so driven to succeed in his field he'd lost sight of everything else.

His father glanced unsubtly at his watch. Time was money—every minute was assigned to some client's account. Daniel geared up to go—realising communication on a level other than work was never going to be part of his relationship with his father. He started to wonder that if he hadn't done law, he'd ever have had a thing to talk to him about.

Time. His mother had wanted more of it—from his father. Said she wanted someone who had time to laugh with her, to love her.

He'd been following in his father's footsteps for so long, been so determined to succeed, he hadn't really understood.

That evening he sat in his apartment not wanting to go to the bar, but illogically wanting to see Lucy. Increasingly uneasy, he looked around his lounge. Lucy's possessions were taking over. Her shoes. CDs stacked untidily by his stereo. He went and looked at the pile. More country. He put the top one in the stereo and pressed play. Listened for a couple of minutes before wandering around the room and breathing in the scent of Lucy. He wished she were home, then wished he didn't wish at all.

He stepped into the hall and peeked through the open door of her room—not sure why he was feeling so reticent given that she slept every night in his bed. Her cowgirl boots were lying on the floor. She must be in sandals tonight—given that it was hot and humid, this was hardly surprising. He smiled at the boots, happily indulging in the memory of the pool table where she had lain wearing nothing but them. Those boots were made for walking. And, yep, he was quite sure they were going to walk right over him.

Probably soon.

He looked at his watch and frowned—near to closing time. He needed to move if he was going to be there in time to walk her home. He refused to have her walk home alone. Bad martial arts moves or not, she was vulnerable. And while she was on his watch he wanted to make sure she was OK.

He walked quickly to the club, foreign anxiety rising in him. He was setting up for a fall here. He wanted Lucy—a lot. More than wanted? His jaw clamped. No, because he knew what to expect—she'd leave. Sooner or later, she'd up and walk out leaving him nursing what—a broken heart? His blood chilled. He'd better end it. He should have finished it with her days ago. That was his rule—finish the fling before she does. But he just couldn't bring himself to—not tonight. Maybe tomorrow.

He woke late again, his brain even more confused. Only knowing that he was pillowed on something soft and warm and he really, really didn't want to move. His eyes jerked open. What the hell was happening to him?

He really needed to do some exercise. He tossed up his options—sex or swim? As if there were any question. But as he watched her sleep he couldn't bring himself to wake her. He fought to resist the urge to run his hands over the tanned curves peeking out at him. He'd love to have her right now but she needed rest. With regret he snuck into the shower at the other end of the flat, dressed and headed to work.

Once back at his office he stared at the email. Damn Lara. He didn't need anything more for his brain to dwell on. Certainly not more Lucy-related stuff.

How long would the transaction take? He had no idea, but he knew he couldn't rely on Lucy to last the duration. She'd never signed on for anything long-term in her life. The minute she found out she'd be off. He knew it in his bones. Somewhere, deep in the chest region, a little spark hoped that she wouldn't. But Daniel didn't rely on sparks. He always, always prepared for all eventualities. Looked at a case from every angle. Broke it down. Decided on his response to each possible scenario—cold, analytical.

He picked up the phone to call a temp agency. He certainly wasn't going to walk into one of their offices—you never knew what you might come across. It didn't take long. A quick outline of what he needed and when he was likely to need it.

After making the call he went to see one of the partners in the commercial arm of the firm. He sent Lara an email back explaining he'd handed over her request to someone else. She was on the phone in a nanosecond. Must have been glued to her BlackBerry.

'What's going on? What do you mean, you can't do it yourself?'

'I can't sell the club for you, Lara.'

'Why not?'

'Because I'm involved…' Ah, he didn't want to go there. 'It's complicated. I do criminal, not conveyancing.'

'Did you say involved?'

'You need to get the best price you can and I need to be out of the negotiations.'

'What sort of involved?'

'Peter is taking over for you. He's the best in the firm and he'll see you right.'

'Are we talking romantically involved?'

'I think you'll find things move quickly. Anyway, those bright lights got to you, huh? You're in Hollywood for ever?'

'Avoid me all you like, Daniel, but you can't lie to your heart.'

Ick. She was on a love high. 'Gotta go, Lara. This is eating into billing time.'

Lara's soft laughter tinkled. 'I can't wait to meet her. Let's do a video conference over the Net.'

'Sure. Next century some time. BYE.'

He hung up. Stared at the phone. Stared at his timesheet. Stared out the window. Horribly afraid Lara was right.

After work he walked slowly to the bar. He didn't want to tell her. This was Lucy—'leave it when the going gets tough' Lucy. She of the goldfish-sized attention span, who'd never held down a job for more than a few months.

The minute Lucy found out the club was going to be put up for sale she'd pack her bags and move on. But Daniel wasn't ready for her to. He wanted to be able to finish with her himself before she departed.

Simple solution. He wouldn't tell her—not yet. An omission, not a lie. He'd buy himself a little more time to slake the crazy lust he had for her.

He was sure it would go. She was like the holiday he hadn't had in a while. That was why he was tempted to come and hang out at her bar. Play pool, sit on the balcony with her and watch the world go by. Spend half an hour reading the paper. Spend a whole hour in bed together and not even doing anything.

He'd ride it out a while longer. Then he'd be back to normal and embracing his overly full schedule again instead of wishing like crazy he could dump half the load and focus on the aspects he really enjoyed.

He rubbed his hand across his forehead, the ache for her burning into him again. It really would fade, wouldn't it? This desire to be with her? Because if it didn't, then he was the one in really big trouble.

CHAPTER FOURTEEN

You make your decisions spontaneously

DANIEL arrived at the bar earlier than usual. He had a look in his eye that hit Lucy's concern switch immediately. Something was up. What?

'Lara's been in touch.'

'Oh, yeah?' Feigning casual interest. Of course this had been going to happen. Only ever a short stint. Just like normal. She'd been chasing dreams. 'She's coming back?'

'No.'

'No?' Her heart started the acceleration process—speedway-style.

'She's…ah…still deciding on her future.' He looked down at the bar, his brow pleated.

'Oh.' She shuffled a couple of coasters. 'So you're needing me for longer than the three weeks, then?'

He nodded sharply. 'Yeah. I'm not sure how long for—play it by ear, shall we?'

Were they talking about her job as bar manager or something more?

She wasn't about to ask. Daniel was a cool player. She'd play it even cooler. Poker face. Hope for the ace. 'Sure.'

Someone to sleep with. That was all he was supposed to be.

But he was no longer a good-looking but two-dimensional suit. He was arrogant but understanding. Tough but gentle. Focused but funny. And she was so far in love with him she couldn't think straight any more. All she knew was that she lived for the nights when, like tonight, he pulled her close and she could pretend to herself that he needed her. That maybe, just maybe, he cared.

As soon as she woke he hugged her to him. 'What are you doing this morning?'

She shrugged. 'I don't know. Maybe go into the club and get ahead on the accounts.'

'No, don't do that. Why not go for a swim? You haven't been in ages.' He swirled a pattern on her stomach with his finger. 'You could meet me for coffee.'

Um. No. She needed to maintain boundaries. Correction. Re-establish boundaries. Carve them in stone. Bed mates. Just good sex. Between utter opposites. Nothing more—and it would be over in the foreseeable future. She didn't do vulnerable, remember? But she was more vulnerable now than she'd ever been in her life.

'I really should get a few things done.'

'Leave the club for a while, go and swim for a bit, have a sauna. Relax.' He smoothed over her muscles as he spoke, heading south. They were far from relaxing, they were gearing up for another round of Daniel's full attention. Excited.

'OK.' It was hard not to agree with anything the man said when he was doing that. She'd agree to anything so long as he didn't stop.

A couple of hours later once she'd snoozed and showered she decided against his advice. She wanted to have the club in top-notch order for when Lara got back. Have the books balanced, the stock management under control and more punters through the door than ever before. She'd got her hopes up that Lara might keep her on. She was comfortable there. It wasn't too big, it was stylish and it was fun. And, yes, she wanted to stay on.

For the first time she wasn't looking to jump ship to another opportunity as soon as one appeared.

Quite where that was going to leave the question of her and Daniel, she didn't know. She was cheerily telling herself the two weren't related—oh, no. Definitely not. She really ought to be moving out of his apartment and into a flat of her own. But she hadn't had a chance to look at the paper or on the Internet. She'd been too busy. Sleeping.

Lucy was staring hard at the computer screen when she heard the key in the lock downstairs. Smiling, she finished the sentence she was on before closing up the laptop, expecting it to be Daniel, her body softening already. Weak, weak woman.

He must have figured she'd be at the club anyway, come to find her for some 'coffee'. They hadn't done middle-of-the-day sex and frankly she was up for it. Anticipation fluttered through her and she couldn't keep it dampened. Whatever happened once Lara did come back, for now she was lost.

But it wasn't Daniel who appeared at the door. It was a man in a suit, but not the one she'd discovered she loved to look at. 'I'm sorry, can I help you?'

'Oh. I was told there wouldn't be anyone here at this time.'

'Really? Well, there is. I'm Lucy, the manager.' She waited to hear who this guy was and why he had a key to her club.

'I'm Peter, the lawyer for Lara, the owner.' He stressed the owner part. 'I'm showing Julia around. She's the agent who'll be handling the sale.'

'Sale?'

Po-faced Peter looked supercilious. 'I thought Daniel would have mentioned it?'

Lucy managed a smile, the sharp-edged snaky sort. 'Yes. I'm sorry, I forgot. I'll hop out of your way.'

'No, that's OK, you might be able to answer a few questions for us. Daniel didn't want you bothered, but if you don't mind?'

'Mind? Of course not.' Why would she mind?

They'd have to chip the smile off her face with a chisel, it was so fixed. Daniel didn't want her bothered? Why hadn't he told her? Lara must have been in touch and told him to sell the club. She thought back to that morning's conversation in bed. He'd been so keen for her to go for a swim. Not to come to the club until this afternoon. Now she knew why. He didn't want her to know. Her mind frantically ate at the reasoning. He hadn't wanted her here when the agent came. Why? Did he think she'd let him down? Not be a good representative for the club?

Usually she was the one to cut and run, but this time the ground had been sliced out from under her. For a split second she thought about heading to his place, packing her bags and hightailing it out of there a.s.a.p. Her gut instinct was to flee. But she pulled herself up sharp. Not. This. Time.

She was good at this job and she wanted to be better. She relished the challenge and loved the responsibility—amazing but true. She finally had a job she felt at home in. She was gutted it was being sold, but she'd show the new owner she was the one to keep on running it. Hell, why couldn't she be the new owner?

She scoffed at her own flight of fancy. As if she'd ever have the money for that. And if she approached a bank they'd laugh her out of town. Credit limit? Hers stood at about twenty dollars.

She'd go find Daniel and ask him what was going on and why he'd wanted her out of the way. For once in her life she was primed to fight, not take flight. She'd finally found something worth fighting for. She headed to the office to get her bag just as the phone rang. She answered crisply. Equally crisp tones responded. 'This is Mona from Hospitality Heroes. I'm trying to track down Daniel Graydon. I'm afraid I've misplaced his number but as this is the bar he was recruiting for I wondered if you could pass on a message.'

Recruiting? 'Sure I can. It was for another bartender, that right?'

'Ah, manager, I believe. I have some very experienced candidates to talk through with Mr Graydon. I'm sure we'll find just the person for him.'

'I'm sure. Thank you. I'll get him to call you, Mona.'

Lucy blinked and slowly replaced the handset. Her brain processed the conversation in slow motion, her heart hammered it home in triple time. Hurt hampered her vision while an invisible boa constrictor agonisingly squeezed breath and life from her heart and lungs.

No.

Experienced candidates...manager.

No.

He wanted to replace her?

No. She pushed at the pain threatening to engulf her and felt her silly hopes plummet as the knowledge sank in. Dreams dashed to smithereens on the rocks of Daniel's ambivalence. He wanted a new manager. So much for playing things by ear. She hadn't even worked through her whole three weeks yet. Was she really doing such an awful job? Hadn't he seen the effort she'd put in? For once she'd given something her all, but she'd still failed. He was a man who gave the best, who expected the best, who frankly *was* the best and who, damn him, *deserved* the best. Her best wasn't good enough—not for him. *She* wasn't good enough for him. Even though she'd known that all along, having it thrust on her like this still hurt.

Her decision to stay and fight faded in a flash. She took deep breaths to blow out the burning anguish inside. Summoned cold anger to replace it. Calm control.

Slowly, pride reared its ugly head. He didn't want her to know? Fine. She wasn't going to fuss or have a flaming piece of him—even though she really wanted to do. She wasn't going to embarrass herself by revealing an overly emotional response to him.

She'd started this cool and she'd end this cool. Just like him. Obviously, as far as he was concerned, it was over. He was looking for a new manager. The bar was being sold. Her days were numbered. He must have caught up on all the sleep he needed. She'd even started to think he might actually have feelings. But, no, he really was cold and heartless. The suit said it all. He wanted rid of her? Not nearly as much as she now wanted rid of him and she'd get in first even if it killed her. She'd do it in super-cool blasé style, not showing even a millimetre of the aching wound stretching deep inside.

What upset her most was his high-handed dealing with the situation. Going completely and utterly behind her back to set everything up. Would he then present it as a *fait accompli?* Oh, by the way, Lucy, your time's up.

How did he expect her to react? Was that part of the game? Well, she wouldn't react. She'd breeze off before he had the chance to play his mean hand. She'd worked so hard on the report and had been dreaming up all kinds of fun things for the club to branch into. Ways of drawing in the right crowds—keeping the vibe cool but a place for good times. As if Lara or the new owner would even be interested? Man, why had she ever imagined they would? She had nothing much to offer them—or Daniel. Nothing that he needed. She had to accept it, deal with it and move on.

She stared at her laptop and blinked back tears. Lucy didn't cry. Ever.

She managed a frigid goodbye when Peter and his agent called out they were leaving and realised she'd need to move fast. Peter would be in contact with Daniel so he'd know she was there and that she knew about the sale. She needed to compose herself before seeing him again.

As for staying and fighting for it? No chance. She'd thought she could put in a mark for the job at the club but he wasn't going to let her. And she'd never grovel. He didn't know she knew about the search for a new manager. She'd keep that one up her sleeve for the right moment. It was time to go home and sort her stuff out. She could be out of there in half an hour if necessary. Fifteen minutes even.

She paused, reconsidering. Working it out. She didn't want to look as if she'd left in a mad fit of pique—there was dignity to consider. Her cool, 'I don't give a damn' response. She needed an excuse.

She mentally flipped open a map of New Zealand. Threw an imaginary knife at it. Daniel's image popped into her head right then and the knife landed in his heart. She screwed up her eyes and abandoned the decision for now. Anywhere would be OK so long as it wasn't here. Better weather—that was it. And she could always fall back on her age-old excuse for up and leaving—boredom. That would get him. Fake reasoning in place, she shut up the club with time enough to get back and pack before having to return for opening.

And there was no way she was sleeping with him again.

To her extreme annoyance he was home when she got there. 'Shouldn't you be at work?'

He looked up from where he was sprawled on the sofa reading one of her magazines. 'Took the afternoon off.'

Dumbfounded she stared at him and then wrenched away, not wanting to be taken in by those golden eyes that seemed to promise the earth. She knew they told other tales behind the light. She tried to keep her movements slow and as natural as possible to hide the tense twitching inside.

'Did you go for your swim?'

She jerked her head in negation. 'Just a walk.'

If he'd taken the afternoon off he might not have seen or spoken to Peter. She'd bluff it.

'What time are you due at the club?'

'Not for another couple of hours.'

His eyes lit up. 'Fancy a rest between now and then?'

Here he was going behind her back to oust her from her job, going to sell the club and not mentioning a thing about it, and still he wanted to sleep with her? When was he planning on telling her? Once he'd had his way another couple of times? Her anger grew to volcanic proportions. The awful thing was, despite the rage she felt there was a part of her that still wanted him. Her weakness made her even angrier. But she reined it in, refusing to blow her stack—that would reveal too much of how she really cared.

'Actually, I need to organise a few things.'

'Oh?' He rose from the sofa and looked at her closely. 'You OK?'

'Mmm.' Not meeting those penetrative eyes, she attempted a casual stroll to her room, keeping her shaking hands in her jeans pockets. She got to her room and pulled her pack from the wardrobe.

'Going somewhere?' He'd silently followed her and now leant against the doorjamb.

'Actually, yeah. I'm thinking it's time to move on.'

'Really.'

'Mmm hmm.' She didn't look at him, kept her mouth firmly closed as she focused on unzipping the bag she'd tossed up onto the bed.

'When do you leave?'

'I'm thinking after the shift tonight.'

'Just like that? No notice?'

She sucked in a quick painful breath. 'Well, it is nearly the end of the three-week trial.'

'I thought you were staying on.'

'No.' She straightened and tucked a stray strand of hair behind her ear. Her fingers brushed her clammy forehead. 'I think it's time to move.'

'It's a little shorter than your usual stint, isn't it? Aren't you usually a three-months kind of girl?'

'I don't think it's working out.'

'Not working out.'

She didn't like the way he spoke, so quiet, measured. It didn't give much indication of his thoughts.

'Lucy.'

'Mmm?' She didn't stop unloading her clothes from the drawer into the pack.

'Look at me.'

Now that she really didn't want to do, because it might just cause her to lose it completely. She wanted nothing more than to yell right in his face. She wanted to shake him—she was so angry. And so, so hurt.

She put a top in the bag.

He stepped into the room, grasped her upper arm.

'Look at me.' His voice was still soft; the pressure of his fingers wasn't.

She reluctantly raised her eyes to his.

'Tell me the truth.'

'The truth is I don't want to be here any more.' And it was true. Not when she wasn't wanted.

'So that's it? It's all just down to what you want, when you want it?'

'Sure.'

His stony façade began to crack. 'What about the club?'

'What about it? Isabel and Corey can manage it between them. You don't need me.' And he didn't. Never had.

'Have you no sense of responsibility?' Volume rising. Anger audible. 'You really are a hedonist, aren't you? Only into something if it's good for you. Not worrying at all about how that impacts on anyone else. What about Isabel and Corey? What about me?' His nostrils flared as he snaked in a breath. 'You don't even care, do you? *Do you?*' His fingers tightened.

She braced and let him throw the accusation, let the pain wash through. She'd sworn never to lie to him, but she refused to lay herself on the line when he'd betrayed her. He could think what he liked. She wasn't going to answer. Couldn't. How dared he be so two-faced? Expecting her to be there for him right up to the moment when he decided he didn't need her any more. Planning to turf her out without even giving her the time to find alternative arrangements.

He took her silence as confirmation. 'Fine. Get your bags. Go.' He flung her arm away, as if touching her had burnt him. His words flew at her, louder and louder. 'Get your bag!' He went to the drawer and scooped up the remaining items, tossing them into the open pack with visibly shaking hands. 'Don't bother with your shift tonight. I can manage fine without you. I don't *need* you!' His face had reddened and his voice roughened. 'You don't want to be here, then go!'

She stared. Mr Cool, Calm and Collected had lost it. His chest rose and fell as if he'd been running endurance for hours. His fists were clenched at his sides. Anger and scorn bled from his pores. *'Go.'* He jerked his head towards the door.

Equally high emotion raged through her. He wasn't even going to try to stop her. Wasn't even going to question why. Well, now she knew for sure. It was over. Well and truly.

Without another word she gathered her bag in both arms and marched out. Not looking back.

Daniel stood rigid in the middle of her room, listened as the front door slammed, and swore. Loudly. Lots. He really wanted to pull something apart with his hands. He'd never felt so angry in his life. He strode out of the room and to the lounge, paced around and swore some more. Overly eloquent Daniel was for once unable to think of a thing to say other than a few four-letter words over and over. Absolute rage ripped through him. She had left him. Up and out without a hint of why, without a speck of fight. His vision clouded in swirls of red. Finally in frustration he pulled back his fist and punched the stainless steel door of the fridge.

He punched hard. The door was harder.

The stupidity of his action was nothing on the stupidity of letting that woman into his life.

The pain shooting up his arm was nothing on the pain crunching up his heart.

He stalked round the room, shaking his hand out, and half stumbled on something. Glancing down, he saw her cowgirl boots lying toe to toe, doing their own mad dance. Mocking him.

He'd known it. As soon as she heard the club was up for sale she'd be off. Out of there faster than a rat in a cattery.

He gulped in air. Wait a second. She didn't know—did she?

As he stared at her boots his brain started functioning again, albeit at a much slower rate than usual. He cursed his hot-headed explosion. That would have to rate as one of his densest moments ever. That and the fridge thing. But he'd been too angry to think. He hadn't been thinking at all. Usually he was able to divorce his emotions from his reason. But all that registered at the time was that she was leaving. Just like that. Skipping out of his life without a care. And it really hurt.

What hurt more was the realisation that he didn't want her out of it at all. The one thing he swore he'd never let happen. Never let a woman get to him. Never *need.*

But Lucy had slipped in—the worst possible person because she'd slip right out again. As she just had.

He had to get her back.

Something must have happened in the morning. Something had made her mad. Something had hurt her. That he had seen. Despite her attempt at indifference, he'd seen the fire in her eyes, the defiance in her chin, the frantic pulse at the base of her neck—emotional as and fighting hard to hide it. He'd been just as emotional and lashed out when he should have been probing. Idiot.

But when it came to Lucy he couldn't seem to think straight—not until right now. He did need her. He needed the peace and comfort he felt in her arms at night. He needed the fire when she teased him through the day.

The thought of her leaving made whatever decisions he had to make seem irrelevant to his happiness. *She* was the key to his happiness. Finally Daniel understood the overpowering need to risk it all.

But she'd just walked out the door to who knew where.

CHAPTER FIFTEEN

You like to have the last word

LUCY couldn't resist. She had to go back one last time to say goodbye.

She phoned ahead and got Isabel. Made sure he wasn't there. Not that there was much doubt about that. Opening time on a weekday night he'd be sitting behind his desk saving someone's world.

She'd been sleeping on a sofa for four nights now, but it wasn't the hunched position she had to lie in that had her aching. It was him. The hurt in her heart radiated out through her whole body.

She walked in and managed a slight smile at Isabel and Corey. The bar was just as she'd left it—no mark of her absence, nothing to show she'd even been there at all. She could safely disappear and not matter. She hated not mattering.

Corey leant on the bar texting on his cell phone. She raised her brows at him. 'On work time?'

He gave her a wide grin. 'You're not the boss now.'

No. She tipped her chin. 'I just wanted to get a couple of things from the office.'

'No worries. Take your time.'

She went in, closing the door behind her. She didn't dare

glance at the small two-seater sofa in there. As it was she was having heated memories of the night she'd taken him there. She tidied a couple of files in the cabinet and checked over the last entries she'd made in the computer. She printed the document she'd written up regarding future events at the club and put it on the desk for whoever was going to take over. She'd put hours into it. They could put it in the rubbish themselves. Picking up her favourite pen, she put it in her pocket, took one final glance around the little empire she'd loved to regard as her own. Then she squared her shoulders and headed back out for the final time.

Daniel stood at the bar. Not sitting in his usual seat but standing right in front of the office door. And of all things he had her cowgirl boots under his arm. They stared at each other until she could no longer stand the accusation in his gaze and looked away first. She glanced over at Corey, whose grin was even wider than before. She didn't need him to tell her it had been Daniel he'd been texting. Men clubbing together, that was what it was. Isabel would never have done that—she was throwing Lucy an apologetic look.

'I'd like a word.' Daniel marched past her through to the office. Every hair stood on end as his arm brushed hers on the way past.

Not wanting a scene in front of the others, she turned and followed him, shutting the door. There was a moment's silence and she became aware the music in the bar had unsubtly been turned up.

'You know the club's up for sale.' He still had a firm grip on her cowgirl boots.

She stared anywhere but at him.

'You go from being happy in my bed, happy pulling pints here to walking out just like that. There had to be a reason—I forgot to ask the other day because I was feeling extremely angry.' He put her boots on the table between them. 'Once I calmed down I realised something had to have happened, that was the logical thing. Am I right?'

'Possibly. Does it matter?'

'Of course it matters. It clearly matters to you.'

'Not really, Daniel.' Which was a major understatement, but if he could be clinical and detached, so could she. 'It's time for me to move on.'

'Really?'

She nodded, not trusting that her voice wouldn't betray her wobbly innards.

'What about us?'

She steeled. 'What about us? It's just an arrangement, isn't it, Daniel? Bed mates—providing a little relief for each other to ensure a few hours' sleep.'

His face grew rigid. 'Of course.' His hands went into his pockets, distorting the line of his immaculately tailored trousers. 'So you found out the bar was going up for sale and decided to skip it.'

'Actually it was because you were looking for another manager that I realised the time was right for me to leave.'

There was a sharp silence. Finally he asked, 'How do you know that?'

'The agency rang while I was here. They'd mislaid your number and called the club directly.' She folded her arms tight across her body and clenched her fists into her sides. 'Just when were you going to tell me my services were no longer required? Did you want another round of sex first?'

'Lucy.' Not conciliatory. Cross.

'You don't think I'm doing a good enough job, do you? You've been sitting at the end of that bar night after night just watching, waiting for me to stuff up. Judge, jury and executioner. What was it I did, Daniel? What rule or regulation did I break?'

'Don't make out like you're some sort of failure, Lucy. It's beyond time you lost that chip. You're not that much of a rebel. It's not like you left school early and descended into some drink and drugs hell.'

'Yeah, that's me. Second-rate rebel.' Second rate all round. Clearly the only thing he thought she was good at was sex. Well, so what? You didn't need to be much of a success at anything to manage that and it wouldn't be long until he found someone else to be as physical with. Her stomach convulsed, revulsed at the thought, but she quelled it—swallowing the nausea. She'd tried so hard. And he hadn't believed in her. He never had.

She was so far out of his league—she knew it and he knew it. Lust was the only reason he was with her and that was transient.

It hurt. Really hurt. She'd hoped that he'd seen the work she'd put in. Thought she'd impressed him. It was pathetic that she wanted to. Since when did she care what some guy in a suit thought? But he wasn't just a suit. He was special. And if he'd believed in her then she'd really have done it—found her place at last.

He frowned at her. 'I think you're doing a great job here, Lucy.'

'Rubbish, Daniel. You wouldn't be looking for another manager if you did.'

'I was worried you were working too hard.'

'Oh, please. That's ridiculous coming from you. I was handling it fine and you know it. That's the most pathetic reason. You just wanted someone else. Be honest.'

'OK. I thought I had better find a replacement. And you want to know why?' He stepped closer. 'Because I knew the minute you found out that the club was going on the market you'd be out of there. Because you've never stuck at anything your whole life, have you? One sniff of anything getting remotely complicated and you'd be gone.' His volume increased. 'And wasn't I right? That's exactly what you did the minute you found out the club was being sold.'

'Actually, you're wrong, Daniel. Wrong. Maybe I would have

done that before. But not this time. For once in my life I was going to stay and fight for that job. I love it. I don't want to leave. I thought I'd see if I could get the new owner to keep me on. It wasn't until I found out about your hunt for a manager that I decided to leave.' She stopped for a quick breath. He looked shocked. 'Because now we know what you really think of me. And I can't say I blame you. That's fine. I never expected you to believe in me.'

'Lucy.'

'Let's leave it. No analysis, remember?' She looked away, not wanting to hear him try to defend something that was simply, painfully true. There was nothing he could say that would put a gloss on it that would make it palatable for her. 'I really think I should go now.'

'Where are you going?' He didn't even try another argument.

Her heart shredded. 'I'm not sure yet. Maybe north. Somewhere warm.' Because she felt so cold inside.

He made a move as if he was going to reach for her and she backed off quickly, opened the door. 'It was fun, Daniel. That's all it was ever meant to be.'

She didn't look at the others as she left. Just put her head down and tripped down the stairs as fast as possible without falling and breaking her neck.

Daniel remained in the room. Immobile. Stared at her cowgirl boots still on the table. After a moment he looked around the small office. It was so different from the day he'd walked in when he'd found the old manager slumped behind the desk drunk and drowning in an array of papers and bottles. Not only had she come in and run it, she'd tightened it—the shelves were stocked with neat files, books, regulations, supply brochures neatly stacked. The desk cleared, the staff roster neatly written up on the whiteboard on the wall. Contact numbers of bar staff alongside. He picked up the paper draped over the keyboard. Scanned the first couple of paragraphs—a report on the club and future prospects. He couldn't read on. Bad feeling prickled. The bruise on his hand ached. She had been doing a good job and she'd wanted to keep working there.

He'd been wrong. It wasn't because of the club's sale that she was leaving. It was because of him. She thought he was finding a replacement because she wasn't doing a good enough job, because he thought she'd leave.

She'd looked so defiant. Bristling but so hurt. Vulnerable underneath the spiky exterior. He'd wanted to prune away the prickles and caress away the pain. Pain that he'd caused.

She cared. More than cared. But was all that emotion because of her love for the job, or love of him? He hardly dared hope for the latter. He hadn't done a lot to deserve it.

Daniel had never felt such insecurity. It wasn't a nice feeling. And nor was knowing she thought something that wasn't true. She didn't think he believed in her? He smarted at the injustice. Why the hell would he have given her the job in the first place if he hadn't? He'd given her the keys to the club, to his home and to his heart. Although she didn't know about that last one. He'd only recently discovered it himself. And he knew that, Lucy being Lucy, there was nothing he could *say* to convince her.

His brain revved into top gear—this was one case he was absolutely determined to win. He'd prove beyond any kind of doubt exactly how much he believed in her.

CHAPTER SIXTEEN

Intense emotions strongly influence you

'WHY don't you go and see him?'

'Who?'

'Daniel.' Sinead glanced at her from between her legs as she performed some scary stretching exercise. 'You know he's been in the bar every night this week. Sitting there. Looking grim. Scaring away the customers.'

'Has he?' Lucy hoped she sounded uninterested. 'You haven't told him I'm here, have you?'

It was time she moved. Sinead's sofa wasn't that comfortable. And despite the fact they'd rekindled their friendship working together, Lucy still felt bad for imposing on her. But she couldn't seem to drag her sorry self away. She took a risk and walked past the bar. Every muscle clenched when she saw the small 'for sale' sign in the door window already had a red 'sold' sticker stuck across it. It would probably have a name change and be turned into some karaoke bar. What did she care? That was the death knell. Because she did care and she couldn't stay in Wellington with him here. She packed her meagre belongings into her beat-up blue car. She'd go to another city, get a job, earn money and open her own club one day. And stay single. For ever. Because she was never putting her heart in this position again.

She flipped though her ancient tapes and wished she hadn't accidentally smashed her MP3 player. Finally she found an old one that she could cope with, jammed it in and turned the volume up loud. Her car spluttered up the hills and coughed round the corners. Nervous about its life force, she turned the stereo and air con off to allow all power to be directed to the engine.

She finally saw the sign for Martinborough. Wine town of the North Island. She'd grown up in the wine town of the South Island—Blenheim. She drove slowly, enjoying the perfect uniformity of row upon row of vines. There'd be some work here she could handle—at least for a while. Sell some wine to some tourists in one of the many vineyard cellars, or waitress in one of the restaurants. Sommelier season—she'd done it on numerous occasions and had reams of experience.

She pulled in and parked along the main street. It was only eleven in the morning and a hot sunny day, but she felt tired and jaded and heartsore. She'd do the rounds tomorrow and look up old employers to see which one she wanted to revisit for a couple of months. She wasn't up to a bright-eyed sell-yourself routine just yet. She went into the supermarket and picked up a couple of items from the deli and bought a bottle of water. She walked down to the grassy square where at festival time crowds came and enjoyed food and wine and conviviality. Today there were a few people dotted around eating lunch in the shade of the trees. She found a vacant spot and spread her jacket out, using it as a rug. She picked at the bread, cheese and salami and eventually gave up in favour of a lie down, closing her eyes in an attempt to doze.

It was a bad idea because all she ever saw when she closed her eyes at the moment was Daniel. All she felt was the memory of his body, his smile, his sparring…and his intensely perceptive eyes. She lay, eyes closed, daydreaming of him. Holding onto the picture of him at peace and laughing beside her. Inside her. Preferring her life in a half-dream where things were right and she was with him, to opening her eyes and the reality of being alone.

She swatted at the fly tickling her cheek. It landed again. She waved her hand again, opened her eyes. Looked straight into gold.

Daniel crouched on the grass next to her, his face leaning over hers, a blade of grass between his fingers—her annoying fly.

He looked sombre. 'You don't need me to help you sleep any more.'

She jerked up to a sitting position. Had she just conjured him up from her imagination? No, he really was sitting there.

'How the *hell* did you know I was here?' Had he put some kind of tracking device in her car?

'I have friends in the force. They were keeping an eye out for your car.'

Worse than a tracking device, he'd set the cops after her. 'That's an abuse of power.'

'You were lucky they didn't pull you over and order you off the road, there was so much blue smoke coming out of the exhaust.'

'What a waste of police resources. I'm amazed you asked them to do it.'

He sighed and flicked the blade of grass from his fingers. 'I'm not here to argue with you, Lucy.'

'Aren't you? It's what we do best.'

'Like hell. This is what we do best.'

He pushed her back on the grass and planted his lips on hers in one movement.

Despite the force of his body pushing her down, his lips were gentle, testing her. She couldn't stop her answer anyway. Pleasure, delight, sad longing.

He ended it just as it hit hot.

She pushed him back and sat up again. 'Why are you here?' She sounded defensive, trying to cover up her desperate desire.

'I've got a proposition for you.'

Forget her heart accelerating speedway-style, this time it was as if he'd hit the blast-off button and her heart were the rocket rapid-firing to Mars.

'What kind of proposition?' Could he hear the way it was beating? She could hardly hear herself speak above the thump in her ears.

He was still for a moment. 'I'm needing a bar manager.'

Job. It was job-related. Her heart slammed down to the heels of her cowgirl boots. Or would if she were wearing them. As far as she knew he still had them. So it was to the soles of her sandals that it sank, squashed.

'You see—' his smile was slightly self-mocking '—I find myself with this bar to look after and I need someone to manage it for me.'

'I thought it had been sold.'

'It has.'

'So how come you're still worrying about it?'

'Because I bought it.'

'What?'

His smile widened. 'I bought it.'

She sat up, jaw hanging a mile open. 'You bought Principesa? Why did you do that? How did you do that? Do you just happen to have half a million sitting in the bank or something? Did you just fancy a new business?'

'I like it. I like being there.'

'Haven't you got enough on your plate?'

'Probably. But I'm a man who likes a challenge.'

She clamped her mouth shut as she absorbed what he was saying. He'd bought the bar. And he wanted her to run it. She should be happy. She should be saying, 'Fabulous, yeah. I'll be there.' But it was all wrong. Something major was missing.

She felt sadder than she had in all the days just past and felt the sting of tears threatening.

Sure, he still wanted her. But just as his bed mate? His sleeping pill in human form?

Not good enough.

She didn't want to be his modern mistress. She didn't want a casual agreement between two consenting adults. What was happening to her? She'd come over all fairy tale and knight on white charger and she wanted *happy ever after.* She didn't want to be his bed partner for as long as he felt like it. Have him finish with her when he was bored and leave her working in his bar and having to watch him with other women. And there would be other women. She'd been wrong about him. Sure, he wore a suit, but in no way was he boring. He was so attractive. He was offering her the job of her dreams but she couldn't do it. The price was too high.

'Um. Thanks for thinking of me, Daniel, but I'm afraid I can't.'

He scrutinised her relentlessly. 'Why not?'

How did she answer that without giving herself away completely? She focused on a patch of the grass about three feet away. 'Um.' Help, brain, think!

'Does it help if I tell you that I bought the bar because I believe in you? That I believe you can run it better than anyone? And that I believe you can stick at it?'

No, it didn't help. Because she had no desire to stick at that particular bar unless she also had his heart well and truly won.

'I'm sorry, Daniel, but…'

'But what?' he whispered.

She looked up at him then, compelled to honesty by his nearness and warmth. 'It's not enough.'

The expression in his eyes was not one of disappointment or anger. It looked a lot like victory.

Completely confused, she scrambled to her feet, wishing she could be bad enough to leave the remnants of her picnic and run, but some rules she just couldn't break—no littering, for one. She stared at the mess of wrappers and didn't know what to do.

He stood. Put his arms around her. A loose prison that she knew she could escape from if she wanted. If she had the strength. She took a half-hearted step away.

'Tell me you don't want to stay,' he whispered again in her ear as his arms pulled her back to him.

She wouldn't lie. Had promised. And he meant everything.

He whispered again. 'Tell me you don't want *me*.'

He knew. Oh, God, he knew. That she was his and that she was wanting to run away because she couldn't deal with having him but not having all of him. Not wanting to live life in the shadow of a ticking clock.

He stepped closer. His arms tightened around her, the length of his body setting her own alight. It was a fire she couldn't cope with any more. Catching her eyes with his, he wouldn't let her break away. The old challenge. He spoke again, his voice low but clear. Heartbreakingly clear. 'Tell me you don't love me.'

She stared back at him in horror. Tears welling. The sob rose and she only managed to stop half of it escaping. She squeezed her eyes shut, tucking her head down and away from him, unable to do the same with her body because he held her to him so tightly.

His whisper in her ear crushed her. 'Why are you doing this, Lucy?'

'Daniel…' Her voice failed as her emotion cracked open.

'Tears? Not from you. Not from my feisty, free spirit.'

But they streamed down her face as he kissed her neck, sweeping aside her wild hair, bending her back so he had access to her throat—so he could brush his lips against it.

'I won't let you do it. I won't let you go.'

She felt shattered because he wouldn't. Devastated because it wouldn't be over until he said so. And she would live in the shadow. It would be slow torture. 'You have to. Please.'

His grip tightened. His hand twisted in her hair as he held her face up to him. 'No.' His kisses moved across her jaw. Tasting her tears.

'Why?'

'Why do you think?' His other hand slipped from her waist to her bottom. Pulling her hard against his groin. Hot. Hard. Primed.

'You want me.'

He lifted his head. 'I do.' He kissed her cheekbone.

It wasn't enough. It would fade. And she wanted more. So much more.

But he kept kissing. And talking. 'I want to have you.' He kissed the other cheek. 'To hold you.' He continued kissing, punctuating his words. 'From this day forward. Sickness. Health. Richer. Poorer. I'll always want you.'

She slackened against him. 'Daniel. What are you saying?'

'Don't you get it, Lucy? I'm not letting you go. Ever.'

'But you don't believe in marriage. Or commitment.'

'I'm thinking it's an institution not unlike the law. Not perfect, but if we work within the system we can make it better.'

Her body started trembling, top-to-toe uncontrollable shaking that she tried to hold back, because she couldn't believe what was happening. What he was implying.

He spoke again. 'You can say it or not. It doesn't matter. But I know.' His arrogance endearing yet terrifying. 'You love me.'

She stared. Couldn't speak, couldn't even swallow. The lump in her throat was that huge.

His smile broke into monumental proportions. 'You do. And I can't live without that love.' His eyes gleamed, hot gold pouring out brilliant light.

Entranced, she gazed at him. Beautiful. Gifted. But a lover to whom she had no right—she wasn't right for *him.* The full force of fear flooded her—love, doubt, despair. This was a mistake that might scuttle his career.

So she loved him. Someday she'd get over it. 'The answer's still no. I won't come back to the bar.' She inhaled deeply. 'Or you.'

CHAPTER SEVENTEEN

You find it difficult to talk about your feelings

HE FROZE. Sound finally emerged, half strangled. 'I *need* you, Lucy.'

'You need me like you need a hole in the head. Come on, Daniel. Aside from sex we have nothing in common.'

'That's not true. We both can't get to sleep at night. Not without each other.'

'We have nothing in common in the things that really matter, Daniel.' She pushed him away. 'You're so much more… worthy than I am. You're living this life where you're going to make a difference. You're an achiever. Someone who'll make the world a better place. You should be with someone similar. Someone like Sarah—who has beauty and brains to match yours.'

'Your belief in me is flattering, Lucy, but I'm just another lawyer—there are thousands of us graduating every year.'

'That's not true, Daniel. You're special and you know it. Why else are they all clamouring for you? Daniel—be a partner! Daniel—be a professor! Daniel—be the Chief Justice!'

'So?'

'So you can't be with someone like me. A guy who's maybe going to be a judge one day can't have a barmaid for a girlfriend.'

'Why not? And I don't want you for my girlfriend. I want you for my wife.'

'Daniel.' Pleading for him to stop offering her the moon when she couldn't accept it. She loved him but she wasn't what was best for him.

'Lucy. You have talents too. You have amazing talents.'

'Like what? Playing second violin? Come on. I'm nowhere near your league and you know it.'

'I know that no one runs that bar better than you. I know that you get those bar staff working and happy. You get punters coming back in those doors time and time again. Since you started there the sales have gone way up. You know how to entertain people, Lucy. You make an environment that people can relax in. That's just as important as winning someone's case for them.'

He read her 'yeah right' expression.

'It is, Lucy. What's life without pleasure? It can't all be hard work. I love my work—you know I do. But I need to relax too—I understand that now. And I need you to help me relax.'

'It's the sex again. That'll fade. You'll get bored soon enough.'

'I will not. And it's not just the sex—we're better than bed mates. You challenge me. You pull my head in when it's sticking out too far. You make me laugh. You point out the fun things when I'm too busy with my head in books. You make my life *real,* Lucy.'

The shakes were back and worse this time. Daniel was in winning-lawyer mode and his arguments were wearing her last shred of resistance down.

'Daniel…'

'Look, on the one hand you're crediting me with a brain and the next you're saying you know what's best for me. *I* know what's best for me. And that's you.' He paled. 'I cannot go through another week like this, Lucy. I cannot be without you. Anyway. I'm not going to be a judge. I don't want to be a judge. Never have.'

'What are you going to do?'

His arms were around her again, smoothing down her back; she knew he could feel her shaking, knew he was being gentle to calm her.

'They're offering me a position at the university—lecturing with guaranteed time for research. I want to study, Lucy. It's where my heart lies. I've never been able to leave that university. You'll be pleased—I'm teaching evidence and ethics.'

She leant into him. 'I feel sorry for your first-years.'

'Why?'

'They'll all fall in love with you.'

He shook his head. 'Not everyone sees me the same way you do.'

She didn't quite believe that.

His hands kept smoothing her ruffled skin, her rocky emotions. 'My office door will always be *open.* I'm going to be the coolest professor on campus with a wife who runs the coolest bar in the city.'

She stood rigid for a second longer. Then with a soft sigh she slipped her arms around his waist. Held him back. His ability to always have the right answer was going to drive her crazy. But how she loved him for it. They stood together—relaxed, relieved—for the ten seconds until the tension rose to the surface again. He pulled back, his hand running down her arm to take her hand. 'We're taking my car. It's much more reliable.'

He held her hand tightly and marched ahead. She almost skipped beside him. Feeling like the most over-excited kid. But still trying to play it cool. Just a little.

Then they got to where she'd parked her car. She stared at the car behind it—that he'd just unlocked. 'Daniel. Your suits are black, your shirts are white and your car is *grey.*'

'So?' He flipped her a fabulous grin that had her insides softening further. 'You provide the colour in my life, Lucy. More than enough colour.'

She slipped into the front passenger seat, shoving her cowgirl boots to the floor.

'You're putting those on for me later.'

She had to stop thinking about that. It would be at least an hour and a half until they were back in Wellington, back in his bed.

But he didn't turn the car and head for the main road back to the city. Instead he took a side road, roaring along and turning into the driveway of one of the more exclusive vineyards.

She looked at him. 'Wanting to stock up?'

'We're staying here.'

'Here? You booked this already?'

'I have a secretary and I've got to make the most of her before I hit the university and under-funding. She booked it half an hour ago once I figured out where you were heading.'

He pulled the car up in front of the main building, disappeared for a few minutes and then came out again, walking quickly. It registered that he looked more dishevelled than she'd ever seen him. His shirt unbuttoned, the tails flapping free of his trousers, a wild look in his eye. And she knew they wouldn't be waiting more than another—oh, five minutes?

He got in the car again and the shingle crunched as he sped down the lane between the vines to the far end of the property. To the sheltered hedge-hidden farm worker's cottage that stood there. He got out of the car, grasped her hand and together they ran.

The cottage was almost decrepit-looking from the outside, but the overflowing well-tended flowerpots gave away its secret within—the care and work that had gone into refurbishing it into luxury accommodation. Warm muted colours, clean lines, a single bedroom with a giant bed. That was really all she noticed.

'There's a bath outdoors apparently, hidden by the hedges. We'll check it out later, right?'

'Oh, yes.'

He walked towards her. Eyes burning. 'I haven't slept in days.'

'Nor have I.'

'Think we should catch up a little now?'

'Definitely.'

The kiss was full and deep and after a mere moment he pulled back and started yanking his clothes off. She followed suit. It was faster to do her own. But she couldn't resist teasing him as they stripped. 'Peanut M&M's or plain?'

'Plain.'

'Mayo or vinaigrette?'

'Mayo.'

'Sunny-side up or over easy?' She mock slapped his arm as the look on his face turned wicked. 'Skip that one. Surf or ski field?'

'Ski field.'

'Cork or screw cap?'

'Cork.'

'Let's face it. We're totally incompatible.'

'Totally.'

'Fast or slow?' She answered before he could. 'I want fast.'

'I want slow.'

'Tell you what, you go slow and make me go fast.'

'Get you across the finish line and you can go round in a victory lap again?'

She nodded. 'Something like that.'

'Sure.' Smiling, he ran his hands down her torso. 'See? We agree on the things that matter.'

'There has to be more than sex, Daniel.'

'There is more than sex. You know that, Lucy. You have from day one.'

'Day one?'

'OK, maybe week one.' He grinned at her. 'We're good for each other. You slow me down at work. I speed you up.'

'Well, thanks very much.' By now they were naked. She pushed and he fell back on the bed with a shout that soon became laughter. She launched herself after him. He wrapped his arms around her and rolled, trapping her beneath him. Then he set about making her go fast—taking his time to enjoy her in ways that pushed her to the limit. He caressed her from top to toe, stroking her everywhere and then right there, while he kissed her slow and deep. He worked her, taking her higher. Moving from her mouth to her breast. She felt him smile, then heard his chuckle as she writhed under him, wanting him to give her the release so badly. But he was in control and delighting in drawing it out for her. Part of her loved it. Part of her was being driven to madness. His fingers rhythmically teased; his mouth nuzzled her breasts. She moaned, on the brink.

He lifted a millimetre away from her and muttered, 'You'll manage the bar.'

'Yes.' She was rewarded with a faster stroke.

'You'll marry me.'

Her throat constricted. 'Yes.' Even faster, so she was even closer.

'Because you love me.'

She expelled a huge breath. 'Daniel, is there going to be some sort of interrogation every time we make love?'

'So you'll admit we're making love.'

With other-world strength she pushed at him so he rolled off her and over onto his back. She quickly straddled him, taking charge. He grinned up at her, utterly unabashed. She stared down, eyes narrowing at the devilry in his gaze. Two could play at this game.

She leant forward and twirled her tongue around his nipple, trying to ignore his hands as they ran over her hips with sensual slowness. She traced her fingers down his hard-muscled chest, feeling it harden more as she did so. His abs clenched into even more defined beauty as she traced over them and then lower. She curled both hands around him, then inched her body down his strong thighs a fraction lower so she could take him in her mouth. She smiled inside as the groan came from deep within him, loving it as his hands rose and he weaved his fingers into her hair.

'Lucy…'

She stroked him and felt him strain up to her. She lifted her head. 'Repeat after me… Lucy can play country music any time she wants.'

He panted—half-laugh, half-gasp. 'Never.'

She grasped him firmer, took him in deeper and then out again before back in another time. His fingers knotted in her hair. She instructed him again. 'Repeat. After. Me… Lucy…' Her hands kept rubbing in an ever-increasing rhythm.

'Lucy…ah… I love you.'

Her fingers squeezed. 'It's about time you said so,' she whispered, all humour gone.

He sat up sharply. He lifted her face up in his hands so he could read her expression before kissing her hotter and harder than ever before. He pulled his mouth a moment away and the words came out on a harsh wind. 'Don't you know already? I've been so obvious.'

'Daniel!' she squealed. 'You're harder to read than a Russian fighter-jet manual—in Russian!'

'I can't keep my hands off you. I can't stay away from you. I've bought that club for you—what more do you want?'

'Same as you. The words.'

It was his turn to force her back, coming to lie over her, his eyes not leaving hers, his fingers back in her hair, combing it from her face, his thumb caressing her forehead. 'I'll give you more than words, Trouble. Every action, every decision I take now is with you uppermost in mind. I care about you more than anything. More than my job, even.'

'Your job makes you who you are, Daniel. Your drive, your passion for it is part of what excites me about you. Giving that up would mean losing part of you—I never want you to do that.'

He smiled at her. 'Sometimes I work crazy hours.'

She smiled back, turned her head to kiss the inside of his wrist. 'So do I.'

'We can make it work.'

She knew he was thinking of his parents, of their failure to stick together through the stresses of his father's career. 'We will. When I'm too old and ugly to run a club I'll open a diner and serve bacon and bananas.'

His gaze slid from hers to her mouth and she watched in fascination as the gold flecks burned brighter, the brown darkening. His thighs rested on hers, his erection pushing at her. She parted her legs, letting him closer, then she wrapped them around him completely and flexed her hips up at him.

'I'm not wearing a condom.'

'I couldn't care less.' She wrinkled her nose. 'Actually I could, but I just want *you.*'

He hesitated and she smiled. 'I'm on the pill, Daniel. Have been the whole time.'

He looked solemn. 'I never thought I'd want kids. But if I can have one of each with green eyes and crazy hair then OK. In about five years.'

She smoothed away the crease in his brow. 'We'll need to add another two to lessen the burden of parental expectation and not for at least *six* years.'

He sparked with appreciation. 'We'll hammer out the fine details later. Right now I just want to feel you, just you and nothing but.'

She nodded. 'Everything, Daniel. For ever. I trust you.'

The moment of connection was more sublime that she'd ever thought possible. Her breath came in on a high cry. Their eyes met, sharing the intimacy with intensity. Fearlessly revealing feelings, reading reactions.

She let go completely. 'I love you.' It wasn't a whisper, wasn't breathy, but a strong declaration that she meant with entirety.

He tensed, colour slashing his cheekbones. 'Say it again.'

Her eyes widened as she saw the need in his, finally understanding that she had the power to make him happy—or otherwise—as he could her. The last of her cool façade shattered in the heat of him, in the need to show him her love. She wrapped her arms around him as tight as she could, drawing him in deeper with her hips. She passionately kissed her way across his jaw until she could take his mouth with her own. 'I love you, I love you, I love you.'

It was then that he lost it. His body clenched hard, his fingers digging into her rounded flesh, holding her close as he thrust in, deeper and harder and faster and shouting out her name. The joy she felt in her heart at his unrestrained reaction radiated out to her body, tipping her over the edge, into exploding light, shaking heat and finally darkness.

Entwined they lay dozing—fitfully, but dozing nevertheless. She stirred, her mind not letting her body give in to sleep.

'You've really bought the club?'

'Mmm hmm.'

'Because you believe in me.'

He opened his eyes, revealing his ever-alert self. 'I would never have given you the job in the first place if I didn't think you could do it.'

'I thought you gave it to me because you had the hots for me.'

'I told you at the time, you're not my type.'

'You're still not mine.'

He swept his hand from her hip to breast and teased with his fingers so her nipple budded into life. 'I know.'

Her mind leapt to another amusing possibility. 'Are we going to have the reception at the club?'

'Hell, no, Corey will break all the glasses.'

She giggled and then sighed as his fingers continued their teasing touches. 'Is that outdoor bath big enough for two?'

'So the owner tells me. Warm and wet.'

'How about hot?'

He raised an eyebrow; she saw the twitch at the corner of his mouth.

She spoke again with studied ambivalence. 'Sounds like it might be worth checking out.'

He caught her hand as he slipped from the bed, taking her with him. 'Trouble, we've finally found something we agree on.'

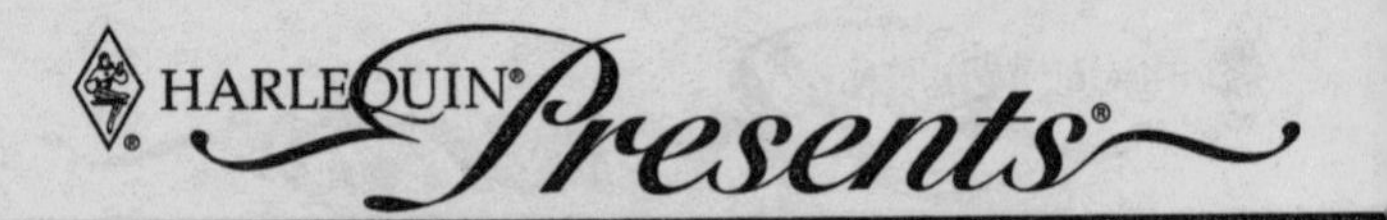

Sicilian by name...scandalous, scorching and seductive by nature!

CAPTIVE AT THE SICILIAN BILLIONAIRE'S COMMAND

by Penny Jordan

Three darkly handsome Leopardi men must hunt down their missing heir. It is their duty–as Sicilians, as sons, as brothers! The scandal and seduction they will leave in their wake is just the beginning....

Book #2811

Available April 2009

Look out for the next two stories in this fabulous new trilogy from Penny Jordan:

THE SICILIAN BOSS'S MISTRESS in May
THE SICILIAN'S BABY BARGAIN in August

www.eHarlequin.com

HP12811

HARLEQUIN®
Romance
New York Times Bestselling Author
DIANA
PALMER
DIAMOND IN THE ROUGH